LOVE IN MONTE CARLO

Within hours of finding herself alone and penniless in Monaco, Eve is rescued by the handsome billionaire Wyatt. She's then caught up in a world of penthouse flats, cutting-edge racing cars, high stakes . . . and low-lifes set on sabotaging, even wiping out, the competition. How will she cope in moments of deadly danger? And will Wyatt turn out to be her most ill-judged romantic choice of all?

KEN PRESTON

LOVE IN MONTE CARLO

Complete and Unabridged

LINFORD
Leicester

First published in Great Britain in 2022

First Linford Edition
published 2023

A catalogue record for this book is available
from the British Library.

ISBN 978-1-4448-4993-6

Published by
Ulverscroft Limited
Anstey, Leicestershire

Printed and bound in Great Britain by
TJ Books Ltd., Padstow, Cornwall

This book is printed on acid-free paper

1

How on earth had they wound up here? Eveline Parker, Eve to her friends and family, mopped the sweat from her forehead and sighed. The harsh sunlight bounced off the sides of the concrete and glass buildings, dazzling her and baking her bare arms and neck.

Despite all the sun cream she had liberally applied before setting foot out of the hotel they could no longer afford, she knew she would burn quickly unless she found some shade.

The straps on her rucksack were chafing at her shoulders. Not surprising, as she had just stuffed everything she owned into it, and it was heavy.

How on earth had they wound up here?

There it was again, that question. Monte Carlo, a name that conjured visions of glamour and fun, rich playboys and beautiful women, the French

1

Riviera, and the holiday of a lifetime.

Eve shaded her eyes with her hand and gazed at the conglomeration of ugly high-rise towers, crammed in a haphazard fashion onto the edge of the land. Where was the old world charm, the cobbled streets, and the quaint French buildings she had expected? This was just a nightmare.

At least the harbour looked beautiful, with the luxury yachts bobbing gently on the water. She imagined herself lying on a sun lounger on the deck of one of those larger yachts, topping up her tan while a waiter served her a gin and tonic. Her handsome, chiselled boyfriend lay on the lounger next to her. It was his yacht, after all. He was a billionaire playboy, she was his girlfriend, and the rest of her life was one long holiday in the sun.

'Eve — are you listening to me at all?'

The harsh tone of Scott's voice cut through Eve's thoughts as he stepped in front of her, pulling her back to the immediate moment. Eve had turned her back on him moments before and stalked away, unable to look at him a moment longer for fear that she might throw a punch at that sanctimonious face of his.

'No,' she said, turning her back on him again. 'Why should I?'

Now she was facing the hotel front-age, a much less desirable view than the harbour. But Scott managed to spoil even that view by trotting in front of Eve once more. His bald scalp had grown red under the sun, and his face dripped with sweat. He glowered at her — or Eve assumed he was. It was hard to tell what expression he was trying to pull when all she could see was her own reflection in his mirrored sunglasses.

'I can't believe you're acting like this!' Scott wiped a forearm across his sweaty brow. 'What's got into you?'

'What's got into me?' That was it, the bubbling mass of anger and hurt boiled over. There was no holding it back. 'You're the one who jumped into bed with that floozy when you told me you had a headache and couldn't bear to be out in the sun today!' Eve jabbed her finger into his chest. 'And now you're accusing me of acting irrationally?'

'Come on, Eve!' Scott held up his hands and took an involuntary step back. 'I didn't mean to, she came onto me and I didn't know what to do!'

Eve placed her hands on her hips and cocked her head to one side. 'Oh — what, like, maybe say 'no thank you, I'm already in a relationship'?'

'It just — it all happened so fast.' Scott mopped at his brow again. Patches of sweat had begun forming on his white T-shirt. Perhaps he had been attractive once, but not today.

Nothing like her imaginary billionaire boyfriend, whom she had decided looked sizzling hot in his swim shorts and nothing else, and yet utterly cool at the same time.

She turned away once more and gazed out at the sparkling blue of the Mediterranean again, wishing that she was out there on one of those yachts. At least she could daydream.

'Eve, you know I love you. That maid,

she was just a stupid mistake. She means nothing to me.'

'Get out of my way, you're ruining the view,' Eve snapped.

'Why won't you listen to me?' Scott yelled.

'Because you're a lying, two-timing snake, that's why,' Eve hissed. 'Now, how many times do I have to tell you? Get out of my life!'

Again she turned her back on him, but this time she began walking. She had no idea where she was going, but anywhere was better than standing here listening to her former boyfriend whining about how his mid-afternoon bout of hanky-panky had been nothing but a mistake.

Mistakes were what you made in exams, not in the bedroom.

Scott trotted up beside her.

'Where do you think you're going?'

'Anywhere you're not,' Eve snapped.

'But where are you going to stay? You don't have any money!'

'Oh right, and you have money, do you?'

'No, but if we stick together, we can work something out, we can find a job or something, or I could phone my parents, they'll help us out.'

Eve quickened her pace.

'Just go away. I never want to see you again.'

'Don't be stupid, Eve, you're making a silly mistake.'

Eve suddenly stopped walking and rounded on him, the weight of her rucksack shifting and almost unbalancing her.

'I'm making a mistake?' She jabbed him in the chest again, hard this time. 'Oh no, I don't think so. In fact, my only mistake has been dating you. My friends warned me about you, but I wouldn't listen. Well, as soon as I get home, I'm going to be apologising to each and every one of them, because they were right; you're a loser, a weak, two-timing weasel, and I'm glad to be rid of you.'

She turned away again. Scott grabbed her arm.

'Let go of me!' Eve hissed, struggling.

'No, I can't let you walk out on me,'

Scott said, tightening his grip. 'It's not fair.'

Suddenly, Eve saw her ex-boyfriend for what he truly was; a needy, immature little toddler. In fact, that was giving toddlers a bad name. She realised that she had been drawing closer to this revelation for a while now. Maybe the impulsive decision to take a year out and travel had been a last-ditch attempt at saving their relationship.

But deep down, she had already known that there was nothing left to save.

Eve managed to wrench her arm free.

'Goodbye, Scott.' She turned her back on him and walked away. Her back tingled at the thought of him watching her leave. Would he chase after her again? How long would it take him to realise they were finished, that she wasn't going to change her mind?

Eve had to fight hard to resist the temptation to look back. If she did, he would surely take that as a sign of encouragement and follow her again. She darted down the first street she came to that took her off the Avenue J. F. Kennedy, with its rows of boutique shops and its beautiful view of the harbour. With no idea of where she was headed, she walked.

Tears prickled at her eyes. Not for Scott, though. Now that she thought about it, he had done her a favour, canoodling with that maid. He'd forced her hand on a decision she should have made a long time ago. No, the tears were for herself. Here she was in Monaco, home to some of the wealthiest people on the planet, the location of all those Hollywood romantic comedies she so loved, and she was miserable and penniless.

She didn't even have enough money for a room for the night, let alone a flight home to the UK. She could phone her parents; they would send her money for the next flight to London, without batting an eyelid. But she wasn't going to do that. She couldn't bear the thought of all the finger-wagging and the refrain of 'I told you so.'

That would be unbearable.

Maybe she could get a job. Waitressing at a cafe, perhaps. But with the extortionate price of rooms in Monte Carlo, she would be lucky if her salary even covered her rent.

Eve stopped walking, balled her hands into fists and screwed her eyes shut.

I mustn't cry! Not now, not here! She clenched her teeth and held back the tears. It would be all right. She had to believe that.

A hand slipped over her shoulder.

'Don't cry babe, it's going to be OK.'

Scott! He'd followed her after all.

'Get away from me!' Eve spun round, planted her hands on his chest and shoved him away.

Taken by surprise, Scott staggered and almost fell over. 'Hey, watch what you're doing!'

'Stop following me!' Eve had to resist the urge to scream at him. She didn't want to cause a scene and start attracting a crowd. But when she glanced at her surroundings, she realised they were on a main road, at a traffic island.

Luxury cars whizzed past them. No one was taking any notice of the couple on the sidewalk.

The sweat running down Scott's bald head had almost turned into a river. And his face had turned bright red. Eve had the feeling that not all of it was due to the heat. He was angry. She didn't need him to take off his mirrored sunglasses so she could see it in his eyes. The ugly twist of his mouth, his posture, all of it screamed a furious, barely controlled resentment.

'Please, Scott, it's over.' Eve hated the tremble in her voice. 'We're finished now, can't you see that? We were finished a long time ago, it's just taken me time to realise it.'

Scott grabbed her wrist and squeezed. 'No, no! It's not over.'

'Ouch!' Eve cried out. 'Scott, let go, you're hurting me.'

He pulled her close. She could smell mint on his breath, and underneath that, the hint of stale cigarettes. Did he smoke? How did she not know that? The heat emanated from him like a furnace.

'You are not going anywhere.' He had lowered his voice. 'You can't, I love you.'

'You're scaring me now.' She tried to pull away, but Scott had grabbed her other wrist and he was too strong for her. 'Please let me go.'

'Not until you tell me that you won't leave me. Tell me you love me still, then I will let go of you.'

Eve tried dragging herself free of his grip, but it was pointless. Scott pulled her even closer and wrapped his arms around her, pinning her to him.

'Come on, babe, you know you're being silly. Stop resisting, give in, you know it makes sense.'

Eve twisted her head away as he leaned in to try to force a kiss on her. The smell of him repulsed her. She struggled to wrench herself free, but he had pinned her arms to her sides and he was too strong for her.

Through her panic, Eve vaguely heard the rumble of an engine and then a car door slamming.

'All right, mate, let the lady go.'

Scott released her and Eve staggered back, out of his reach. She turned to look at the man who had spoken. He was tall, with tousled blond hair, blue eyes, and a strong jaw. Pretty much the definition of drop-dead-gorgeous, Eve couldn't help thinking, despite the tension of the situation.

He was standing by his car, a sleek, midnight blue convertible, the engine still running. His hands were by his sides and bunched into fists. From the look on his face, Eve suspected he was about ready to use them.

Scott eyeballed the blond man, getting in up close and trying to intimidate him. 'Look, mate, this is none of your business, all right?'

Blondie was having none of it. He was wearing a fitted overall with the names and logos of racing car companies printed on it. Eve thought he must be hot inside there. But if he was, he didn't show it; he looked as cool as a cucumber.

He flashed a smile at Scott, but it wasn't a friendly one.

'Sure it's my business when I see a young woman being bullied by a guy twice her size. Now, do you want to walk away and save yourself a hiding, or would you rather do this the hard way?'

Scott jutted his jaw out and stared up at the man. 'Yeah? Think you can take me, do you?'

In one swift movement, the man reached out and pulled Scott's mirrored sunglasses off his face. He tossed them casually to one side.

'Don't be silly,' he said. 'Not so brave now, are you, when you can't hide behind those?'

All of a sudden, Scott didn't look so sure of himself. He blinked in the sunlight. The belligerence melted away like ice-cream in the heat. He muttered something and shot a glance at Eve. He picked up his sunglasses and put them back on.

With one last look at Eve, he stalked off.

'Thank you,' Eve said as she watched Scott turn a corner and disappear from view. All of a sudden, the tension and panic drained from her body, leaving her feeling a little giddy.

'My pleasure,' her rescuer said. He threw her a smile, a much friendlier one than he had given Scott. 'My name's Wyatt, and you are?'

'Eve.' She held out her hand, and they shook.

'And who was that waste of DNA that was bothering you?'

'My ex-boyfriend.'

'Seriously? Wow, you know how to pick them, don't you?'

A sudden indignation flared in Eve's chest.

'What's that supposed to mean?'

'He's a creep, it was written all over his face. What did you even see in him in the first place?'

Eve had just been wondering herself, but she wasn't about to let Wyatt know that.

'Well, I think that's none of your business. Thank you for your help, but I must be on my way.'

She turned on her heel and began walking.

'Wait a second,' Wyatt called after her. 'Where are you going? I can drive you there if you like.'

'No thank you!' Eve called over her shoulder. 'I'm perfectly capable of looking after myself.'

What on earth are you doing? Eve thought. *He obviously wants to help, why not let him? He might know somewhere you can stay for a couple of days, or a way you can earn some money.*

When she heard the car door open and close, a pang of disappointment shot through her chest. He was leaving already? Eve scolded herself for being so proud and fiercely independent. This gorgeous guy had just rescued her from a tricky situation and now she was spurning more offers of help? What on earth was she thinking?

But then he drove up beside her.

'That rucksack looks heavy,' he said, keeping pace with her as she walked.

'It's perfectly fine, thank you,' Eve

replied, not even looking at Wyatt as she spoke. Why did she have to be so obstinate?

'Have you got a place to stay?'

'Of course I have,' Eve said, looking straight ahead to keep her expression from betraying the lie she had just told.

'I'm pleased to hear that, because it looks like it's going to be a hot day, and I wouldn't want to be out here when those temperatures really start to climb. I've seen people just drop down in a faint, their faces lobster red from all that sun, and just lying in a big puddle of sweat on the ground.'

Eve stopped walking and turned on Wyatt.

'You really are charming, you know that? Is this meant to be a chat-up line? Because I have to tell you I don't think I've ever heard a worse one.'

Wyatt grinned up at her from the open-top car, the seats a pale cream colour, wide and luxurious. 'You're looking a little red in the cheeks already. I'd think about finding some shade real soon if I was you.'

'And if I were you, I'd think about learning how to treat a girl a little more politely,' Eve snapped.

'Here comes the next stage, the sweating.'

'What are you — ?'

A trickle of sweat ran down Eve's forehead and into her left eye. She blinked furiously and wiped the sweat away.

'Ooh, you are infuriating!'

'But I'm right, aren't I?' Wyatt grinned at her. 'Come on, get in the car.'

Eve looked at the two-seater, the top down, the display on the dashboard like something out of a science fiction movie. Wyatt looked up at her, a charming smile on his face. It was tempting.

No, it was more than tempting. Here was this attractive man driving the poshest, sexiest car she had ever seen, offering her a lift. And she was refusing him?

'Where would I put my rucksack?' she asked, feeling ever so slightly flustered. It was a stupid question; she could easily sit with it on her lap.

'Believe it or not, there is space in the boot.' Wyatt jumped out and popped the catch. 'See?'

Eve could see. In her mind's eye she could also see herself sitting in the passenger seat of this amazing open-top car, her hair blowing in the breeze, and this good-looking guy driving. It would be a dream come true.

Eve wondered if he had a yacht, too. If he did, then he was definitely a millionaire. Eve remembered her daydream earlier. Perhaps it could come true? How good was he at applying sun lotion? she wondered. Those hands looked —

'Come on, let me drive you,' Wyatt said. 'I'll take you anywhere you need to go.'

And then Eve remembered that there was the problem; she had nowhere to go. She could get in the car, but then what? When Wyatt asked her where to, what was she going to say? The nearest homeless shelter, please?

And then Wyatt would know that she was not only homeless, but she had lied to him too.

Her cheeks must be positively glowing by now. But this had nothing to do with the heat. This was pure embarrassment. Without another word, she turned her back and stalked off.

'Hey, where are you going?' Wyatt shouted.

'None of your business!' Eve called back.

'You really are the most unusual girl I have ever met!' Wyatt yelled.

Eve heard the slam of the boot and then the car engine roaring into life.

'And choose your boyfriends a little more carefully from now on, all right?'

And with that, he was gone, leaving Eve all alone in Monte Carlo.

Her daydream of lounging on a yacht with her millionaire boyfriend vanished like early morning mist. Here she was, in the glamour capital of the world, Monte Carlo.

And she was penniless, alone, and miserable.

2

'What kept you, Boss?' Happy, the chief mechanic said.

'What?' Wyatt Bailey-Kinsey snapped out of his thoughts. 'Oh, some idiot was trying to prove himself in front of his ex.'

'And you couldn't stop yourself from being the knight in shining armour, huh?'

'Shouldn't you be concentrating on making all your final checks on the engine?'

Happy grunted. 'All finished, you're good to go.' He chewed on the long, fat cigar jutting from his mouth. He couldn't smoke in the garage, but he always had a cigar clamped between his teeth, even if most of the time it was unlit. He watched Wyatt with narrowed eyes.

'What?' Wyatt said.

'You've fallen for some dizzy blonde, haven't you? I can see it in your eyes.'

'What are you talking about, you can see it in my eyes?'

Happy chewed on his cigar. 'You've got that faraway look you always get when you meet some girl and she flutters her eyelashes at you. Your tongue will be hanging out next. Well? Am I right, or am I right?'

Wyatt sighed. 'All right, yes, she might have caught my eye, I'll admit that, but I haven't fallen for anyone.'

Happy shook his head. 'You've got to keep your mind on the race.'

'I am keeping my mind on the race. I am completely and totally focused.'

'So how come you looked like a rabbit caught in headlights when I asked what kept you?'

'I was thinking,' Wyatt replied.

'Yeah? What about?' The cigar, seemingly with a life of its own, shifted from one corner of Happy's mouth to the other.

Eve, that girl I just met, Wyatt almost said, but managed to stop himself.

Happy noticed Wyatt stalling and sighed.

'You're gonna lose this race tomorrow,

I can tell you now.'

'Thank you for your vote of confidence.'

Happy tapped his forehead. 'You ain't got the hunger to win any more. You lost it because you met some blonde this morning and now you can't stop thinking about her.' Happy shifted the cigar back across his mouth. 'I'm right, aren't I?'

'Of course not,' Wyatt said, and jerked his thumb over his shoulder. 'Now get out of here. Isn't there something else you should be doing?'

Happy grunted and stalked off, muttering.

Wyatt drifted away on his thoughts again, tuning out Happy and the sounds of the garage. Meeting Eve had thrown him. He couldn't get her out of his mind; Happy was right. When he saw that low-life threatening Eve, Wyatt had to go and intervene. He'd promised himself to keep out of other people's business, but when he saw something like that, it was as though a switch flicked in his head.

But it wasn't the low-life he kept thinking about, it was Eve. He hadn't really noticed at the time, but she was cute. No, that wasn't true, of course he had noticed. And she was more than cute, she was beautiful. If only she had let him give her a ride somewhere, maybe they could have got to know each other a little.

What had he been thinking, criticising her choice of boyfriends? All right, so she had made a terrible choice with that creep Wyatt had pulled off her, but it had still been rude of him to tell her. If Wyatt had just kept his mouth shut, she might have accepted that ride. It probably hadn't helped that he had teased her about the heat, too.

But then he thought he'd turned things around. She had looked ready to get into the car with him until she suddenly turned on her heel and walked off without a word. What had he done? Had he offended her somehow? Was it something he had said, or didn't say?

And why on earth had he shouted after her to pick her boyfriends more carefully? Talk about patronising. He'd been flustered. He couldn't let her leave without saying something, but couldn't he have thought of something better?

Wyatt shook his head. Some days, the opposite sex was a complete and utter mystery to him. Admittedly, that was part of the attraction for him, but some days he wished he was a little more clued in on the mystery.

How did he know she even had somewhere to stay? What if that sleazy ex of hers took it upon himself to have another go? Maybe he should go back into town and look for her.

He didn't exactly have time right now, though, did he? And what were the chances of finding her? Slim to non-existent. Especially with Monte Carlo buzzing with tourists and race spectators.

Wyatt blinked and shook his head again. He just couldn't get her off his mind.

Just when he needed all his faculties to be crystal clear and pin-sharp for the race tomorrow. Was Happy right? Had he lost his hunger to win the annual Alternative Grand Prix, or AGP as it was known, now that he had met a beautiful girl?

★ ★ ★

'So, this is the hunk of junk you think is going to win the AGP, huh?'

The voice cut through Wyatt's thoughts, bringing him back to the present once more.

'Ruggiero, to what do we owe the honour of your visit?' Wyatt said, his tone barely hiding the dislike he had for this man.

The Italian racing driver grinned. He had on his trademark dark sunglasses and his hair was slick and carefully parted. He wore a jacket over a white T-shirt and linen trousers. Rubbing his hand over his carefully stubbled chin, he examined the racing car's gleaming engine.

'You are a fool,' he said. 'These electric engines will never have the sheer raw power of petrol engines. You will drive over the line in last place, my friend. And I will be on the winner's podium, laughing as you limp into the pit.'

'Is that all you came over here for, to gloat? The race isn't for another day yet and you've already crowned yourself the winner.'

Calvino Ruggiero's grin grew wider, and he held out his arms. 'Some of us are natural born winners in life, Bailey, and some of us are natural born losers. Just like your father was a loser and mine is still a winner.'

Wyatt placed his hand on the car bonnet and slammed it shut. 'We'll see, Ruggiero, we'll see. Now, if you don't mind, I have work to do.'

Ruggiero laughed. 'Work all you want, my friend, but you are a loser and you will realise that on Saturday when you crawl over the finish line in last place. That is, if you don't crash first.'

Happy suddenly appeared at Ruggiero's side with a can of oil in his hand.

'Oh!' the mechanic exclaimed. 'So

sorry, Mr Ruggiero.'

Ruggiero stared at the dark patches of oil on his white shirt and his expensive jacket.

'You idiot!'

'I don't know what happened, the oil just squirted out of the can by itself,' Happy said, a look of mock surprise and innocence on his face.

Wyatt rubbed a hand a hand over his mouth to disguise the smirk he couldn't hold back.

'You did that on purpose!' Ruggiero yelled in Happy's face.

The Italian towered over the diminutive mechanic, but Happy was a tough, grizzled veteran of professional racing pit-stops and garages around the world. He knew how to face up to prima donna racing drivers, especially the likes of Calvino Ruggiero.

'Only you would walk into a workshop dressed up like a mannequin in a New York City department store. It was an accident. Is it my fault you weren't wearing overalls?' Happy chewed on his cigar.

'You did this on purpose, and you'll pay for it, I'm telling you!' Ruggiero yelled, sweat springing out on his carefully manicured face.

'Is that right?' Happy said, grinning. The two men glared at each other.

'All right, that's enough, you two,' Wyatt said. 'Ruggiero, send us the cleaning bill for your clothes.'

Ruggiero glared at Happy a moment longer then turned on his heel and stalked out of the cool shade of the garage and back into the sunshine.

A ripple of laughter coursed through the workspace.

'Good one, Happy,' Tig said, chuckling, pushing her fringe back off her face with her forearm. Elijah grinned as he wiped his hands on a rag blackened with oil.

'Cut it out, you lot,'Wyatt said, turning to face Happy and the two mechanics. 'That was pretty childish of you.'

Happy cocked an eyebrow. 'But funny, right?'

Wyatt allowed himself a brief smile.

'Well, yes, maybe just a little.'

'And that was a cheap shot about your father,' Happy said. 'Ruggiero deserved more than a squirt of oil over his fancy clothes for that, he deserved a punch in the kisser. Your dad was the best in the business, and that little creep has no right to talk about him like that.'

Wyatt placed a hand on Happy's shoulder.

'Yeah, I know, Happy, and thanks.'

'Everything all right in here?'

Wyatt groaned inwardly and turned.

'Yes, everything's fine, thank you Mr Sisters.'

'Alrighty then, just checking — the pizza guy didn't look too happy on his way out. And hey, it's Solomon, all right? Or Sol even, but cut out the Mr business, will ya?'

A cigarette between Sisters' lips bobbed up and down as he spoke, a spiral of grey smoke curling upwards.

'Solomon, you can't smoke in here.'

Sisters dropped the cigarette on the

concrete floor, ground it out with his shoe, took off his pork-pie hat and wiped his jacket sleeve across his forehead. His shirt strained at the buttons over his belly and his tie looked as if it might have the remains of his breakfast glued to it.

'Did Penelope send you?' Wyatt said.

Sisters grunted. 'Mrs Bailey-Kinsey said I should keep an eye on things here, yeah. That's what she's paying me for, right?'

Wyatt shook his head in exasperation.

'Look, we're fine. I'm not sure why she felt the need to hire a private detective, it's a little dramatic if you ask me.' He paused. 'No offence.'

'None taken.' Sisters placed his hat back on his head and hitched his trousers up. 'But you can't be too careful, you know. I've been putting out some feelers and I can tell you there's a lot of excited chatter out there about this new, fan-dangled electric engine you've developed.' He took a step towards the car. 'You mind if I take a look? I was a grease-monkey, back in the day.'

Wyatt cast a warning glance at Happy. He knew exactly how the mechanic felt about Solomon Sisters, Private Investigator, and he didn't want a repeat of the squirting oil can incident. Sisters might not wear the expensive clothes Ruggiero favoured, but Wyatt sensed an anger in the private detective that he didn't want stirring to life.

'I'm afraid we're rather busy today, Mr Sisters. Maybe another day,' Wyatt said.

Sisters bowed his head, the brim of his hat obscuring his face.

'Okey dokey. Well, I'll make myself scarce. Give me a yell if you spot anyone suspicious.'

'Will do.'

Wyatt watched Sisters as he ambled out of the garage. Happy pointed at the crushed cigarette.

'What does he think this is, a trash bin?'

Wyatt sighed. 'Who knows, Happy? Who knows? Hey, have you guys had breakfast yet?'

'Are you buying?' Happy said.

Wyatt nodded. 'I'm buying.'

A cheer erupted from the rest of the crew.

'There's your answer, Mr BK,' Tig said.

3

Upon hearing Wyatt drive away, Eve had stopped walking and turned just in time to see his car disappear around the bend on the harbour road. She sighed. There he had been offering her help, and she'd turned him down because of her stupid pride.

She stood still, thinking about her encounter with this man who had rescued her from an awkward situation. He was handsome, that was for sure. He even wore those overalls with style. Eve wondered if he was a mechanic working on one of the cars in the Grand Prix. If only she had let him give her a lift, she could have got to know him a little better. The problem was, though, she had nowhere to go. She could hardly have suggested that he just drive her around for a while until he got bored or ran out of petrol.

There was no point wondering what might have been. The chances of bumping into him again were pretty remote, and she had more important and urgent matters to worry about.

Like, for example, how she was going to find a place to sleep tonight when she had no money? Had Scott got money? He'd said no, he hadn't. But he'd cheated on her with that maid and he'd obviously been keeping a smoking habit from her. What else was he lying about?

And how could Eve have been so blind to it all?

That parting shot of Wyatt's as he drove away, *choose your boyfriends a little more carefully from now on*, had stung. But now that her indignation had slipped away, she found herself wondering if he was right.

Maybe he was, except Eve had never set out to find a boyfriend who would cheat on her and lie. Here she was already thinking about Wyatt, and his tousled blond hair and good looks. But how did she know he was better boyfriend material than Scott had been? For all she knew about him, he could be even worse!

There was no point in thinking about this right now. Any opportunity of getting to know Wyatt better had disappeared when she walked off and refused his offer of help. Best thing to do now was to start working out what she should do next.

Choose your boyfriends a little more carefully from now on!

'Oooh!' Eve groaned in frustration. Why couldn't she get Wyatt out of her head? Especially that parting shot of his.

Even her mother had said as much in the past. No matter how hard Eve tried, she always seemed to wind up with someone who caused trouble. And this was the biggest kind of trouble, stranded in Monaco, one of the most expensive places on the planet to visit, and with no money.

Again, Eve considered phoning her parents and asking for the plane fare home. But that would mean having to tell them about Scott, which would then degenerate into a conversation about how Eve never listened to her parents, and if she would only take their advice and use her common sense, then . . .

Eve blocked her parents' voices from her head. Even if she found the money she needed by other means, at some point she still had to go home and tell them about Scott. There would be more than enough time to listen to them nagging her then, she didn't need them in her head right now.

'Excuse me, Miss, you can't stay here!'

A man in a hard hat and a yellow high visibility jacket approached her, waving her on. Behind him, a vast line of construction vehicles trundled down the road towards them.

'Oh! What's happening?'

'You're standing on the route for the AGP. We're building the spectator stands today, and unless you move I'm afraid you're going to get squashed, and I don't want that to happen because it means I'll have a ton of paperwork to fill out and I'll probably get the sack.'

Eve laughed. 'Well, I'll go then, I don't want to get you into trouble.'

With one last look at the shimmering blue sea, visible in the gap between two hotels, Eve turned and headed into the city. Being forced to move on had shaken her from her reverie and helped her come to a decision. There was absolutely no way Eve was calling home and asking for help. She had got herself into this pickle and she was going to extricate herself from it.

Yes, Monte Carlo was expensive, but surely she could find paid work for a few weeks? There had to be jobs available, especially with the AGP being held in just a few days.

It had been Scott's idea to come to Monaco for the Alternative Grand Prix. He was the car obsessive, not Eve. She had agreed in the hope that they could experience some of the glamour that Monaco promised. That was looking increasingly unlikely now. But still, if she could stay for a couple of days at least, she would like to see the Grand Prix. Although she had no interest in cars, the atmosphere of growing excitement had infected her, especially the thought of seeing all those cars racing through the city streets.

As she walked, Eve looked out for cafes and bars that might need extra staff to cope with all the tourists arriving to watch the racing. The bars were all closed, but she spotted a few that had signs in the windows asking for bar staff. The cafes were open and bustling with activity. Each coffee shop she discovered, she enquired inside about the availability of work. Each one she was met with a shake of the head from the owner; they had all the temporary help they needed.

It seemed Eve wasn't the only one looking for work. At some point later in the day, she would need to circle back to those bars with the 'Staff Wanted' signs in the windows, and hope she wasn't too late to get a job.

After a full morning of wandering the streets of Monte Carlo, her feet sore and her body weary, Eve was about ready to give up. But she couldn't. If she didn't get a job today, then she would have nowhere to stay tonight, and no way of travelling back home.

Tired and feeling a little desperate, Eve spotted a cafe that she hadn't visited yet. This one seemed rowdy though; already she could hear shouts and laughter. What was going on? Did this place serve alcohol too? Were they all drunk?

Eve paused at the door. It was called The English Princess Cafe, which struck Eve as funny because there was nothing remotely reminiscent of an English Princess about it.

Taking a deep breath, Eve stepped inside.

The English Princess Cafe wasn't as full of people as she had thought it would be. In fact, there was only one group of customers, seated around a large, round table and eating what looked like the biggest breakfast Eve had ever seen. They were the ones making all the noise. There was no sign of an English

Princess anywhere.

Eve hurried past them with her head bowed, and up to the counter where an old man perched on a stool, his head nodding on his chest and his eyes almost closed.

'Excuse me.'

The man opened one eye and regarded Eve suspiciously. 'Yes?'

'I'm looking for work and I wondered if you had . . .' Eve's voice trailed off as the man closed his one eye again.

'No work here,' he said, and seemingly fell asleep.

Eve bunched her fists on the counter. That was it then, she'd had enough. She couldn't face another round of rejections later that day when the bars were open. It was all too much.

The only option left was to swallow her pride and call her parents. They would transfer some money to her bank account and she could book a flight home. With a heavy heart, Eve turned her back on the sleeping cafe owner and trudged towards the door.

'Excuse me, can we have more coffee here?'

Eve turned to the speaker, one of the customers crowded around the table, groaning with plates of toast, eggs, bacon, fried mushrooms, and mugs of coffee and tea.

'I'm sorry, I don't work here,' she said.

'Hey, I know you!'

Eve recognised the voice immediately. Wyatt. Her tummy managed a double back flip and a somersault, all in the space of a split second.

He was sitting on the opposite side of the table. He waved her over.

'Come and sit down, you look like you're about to fall down.'

Wyatt shifted up to make room and dragged a chair into the space. As she walked around the perimeter of the group, Eve noticed smiles passing from one person to another as they cast amused glances at each other.

'Cut it out!' Wyatt snapped. 'You lot are like immature school kids.'

Wyatt had changed out of the overalls

she had seen him in earlier that day. Now he wore a white T-shirt, tan shorts and sandals. He managed to look casual and yet elegant at the same time.

Eve sank onto the wooden chair with a grateful sigh and dropped the heavy rucksack beside her. She hadn't realised how tired or thirsty she was.

'Here, have a drink,' Wyatt said, passing her a glass of orange juice. 'Would you like a tea or a coffee? How about some breakfast? This is about the only place in Monaco that serves a full English breakfast.'

Eve gulped at the cold, fresh orange juice.

'Oh no, I shouldn't stay, you're being too generous.'

'Nonsense.' Wyatt turned to the sleeping man at the counter. 'Hector! More tea and coffee, and cook up some more eggs and . . . aww man, just give us more of everything, all right?'

Hector jumped to his feet and scurried through a doorway and into his kitchen.

'Are you sure? I —'

Wyatt held up a hand.

'Shush, you're my guest here. If you continue to refuse my generosity, I shall be offended.'

Eve mimed zipping her lips shut, twisting a key in a padlock and then throwing the key away. A pang of guilt at the way she had spoken to him earlier struck her. She ignored it.

'Much better,' Wyatt said. 'Now, let me introduce you to this ragtag bunch of mechanics and hangers on.' He pointed at a short, bald, thickset man who glowered at Eve as if he'd already made up his mind about her and none of it was good. 'This is our head mechanic, Happy. Say hello to Eve, Happy.'

Happy grunted and, if it was even possible, deepened his frown. An unlit cigar jutted from his mouth.

'Don't mind Happy, beneath that glare of hostility and unfriendliness lies a bitter and twisted old man who despises everybody equally.'

Eve gulped. 'It's nice to meet you, Happy.'

The squat mechanic grunted again, shoved a slice of toast in his mouth, and began chewing. He didn't bother removing the cigar.

Wyatt gestured to a rangy man with a shock of white hair and a long, morose face. 'And this is our lead developer of the new experimental engine we are developing, Elijah.'

'Pleased to meet you, Elijah,' Eve said.

Elijah's face split into a wide, toothy grin and his face was transformed into a friendly, open expression. He reached across the table, his long arm seeming to extend further than was humanly possible, and shook Eve's hand.

'Nice to meet you too, Miss,' he drawled.

'And this,' Wyatt said, gesturing to a young woman with short, black hair, 'is Tig Stubbs, the new recruit to Team Bailey-Kinsey.'

'Hey, how are you doing?' Tig said, giving Eve a warm and welcoming smile.

'I'm good, thank you,' Eve replied.

'Are you a grease-monkey?' Tig said.

'A what?'

'A grease-monkey, a mechanic,' Tig replied. 'That's what we call ourselves.'

'Um, no, I'm not.'

Hector returned with a tray laden down with drinks and began placing them on the table.

'So, I'm guessing you're in the Grand Prix?' Eve said, looking at Wyatt.

'We're not just in the Grand Prix, we're going to win the Grand Prix,' Elijah drawled.

'Not so fast, Beanpole,' Happy growled. 'We've still got a ton of bugs to iron out on the engine's coolant system, and the connectors are playing up, then there's the —'

'Enough already!' Tig shouted, laughing. 'Happy, you've got to lighten up a little, we're going to do this.'

Happy grunted. 'Not if Calvino Ruggiero has anything to say about it.'

'Ruggiero is a blowhard,' Elijah said. 'He's all talk, no action. We'll leave him eating our dust.'

'You mentioned a new, experimental

engine,' Eve said. 'Is that why you're going to win?'

Happy grunted, and Eve wondered if it was a stifled laugh.

'Without wishing to sound arrogant,' Wyatt said, 'I'm hoping we will win because of my driving skills, as well as the wonderful team of mechanics here too, of course.'

'Yeah, whatever!' Tig said, laughing and throwing a screwed up napkin at him.

Wyatt ducked. 'But the point of winning is to show that our new electric engine is capable of enough power and speed to compete with traditional fossil fuel engines in the competitive arena of motor sports. That way we can get the investment to make improvements and start manufacturing at scale.'

'And if you don't win?' Eve said, then regretted how negative she sounded.

'It's back to the drawing board to figure out how we can win the next race.'

'There's something I don't understand,' Eve said. 'Why is it called the

Alternative Grand Prix?'

Hector arrived with a tray of food. Wyatt handed Eve a plate almost overflowing with sausages, bacon, eggs, fried mushrooms and tomatoes.

'Here, eat this.'

More food arrived, racks of toast, fried bread, bowls filled with fried mushrooms and baked beans. Everyone began tucking in, passing the salt, ketchup, brown sauce, teas and coffees.

Eve groaned. 'I might explode if I eat all this!'

Wyatt grinned. 'Go for it!'

But Eve was hungrier than she had thought, and was soon devouring her plateful.

'To get back to your question, the Alternative Grand Prix is exactly what it sounds like, an alternative to the Formula One Grand Prix held earlier in the year,' Wyatt explained. 'You could probably call it more of an amateur racing sport, entered by enthusiasts rather than professionals.'

'Speak for yourself,' Happy said. 'I'm

no amateur.'

'But this year I'm using the race as a pitch for investment in our new electric engine,' Wyatt continued, ignoring Happy.

'Wow, it sounds amazing,' Eve said, munching.

'Maybe you could come and watch,' Wyatt said. 'It would be great to have you there, if you don't have any other plans, of course.'

Eve noticed Happy throwing a glance at Wyatt, but she couldn't interpret it. Did Happy not like her for some reason?

She decided to ignore him.

'I'd love to,' she said.

★ ★ ★

Once they had finished eating and Wyatt had settled the bill with Hector, they stepped outside and back into the scorching sunshine.

'Where are you headed now?' Wyatt said. 'We can drop you anywhere you like.'

'Oh, I, um . . .' The familiar sense of embarrassment and obstinacy reared its head, tangling Eve's words, preventing her from talking.

'You've got nowhere to go, have you?'

'Of course I have!' Eve exclaimed, that silly burst of indignation refusing to let her tell the truth. 'I'm not homeless, you know.'

'Great — so let me drop you off, then.'

Eve felt her cheeks reddening. She'd hoped Wyatt wouldn't notice, but already she could see him grinning at her discomfort. And already she could feel those rucksack straps digging into her shoulders again. Her obstinate pride disappeared, melting like ice-cream in the sunshine.

'All right, if you must know, you're right, I haven't got a room anywhere at the moment, but I'm off to book one right now.'

Happy grunted. 'You believe in miracles, lady?'

'What's that supposed to mean?'

'What Happy is trying to tell you,

in his eloquent manner, is that all the hotels will be fully booked. If you haven't already got a room, you'll be lucky to find a spare park bench for the next few nights.'

'Oh no.'

'Hey, you can bunk with me,' Tig said.

'Really?' Eve replied, the relief flooding through her body. And for once she was ready to accept help from someone. 'Thank you.'

Happy guffawed, shoving a cigar into his mouth.

'What's so funny, Happy?' Tig challenged.

'She's a high-class broad, not a grease-monkey,' he said, the cigar clamped between his teeth as he spoke. 'You think she's really going to want to spend the night in your makeshift excuse for a room at the back of the garage?'

'I'm very grateful,' Eve said, ignoring the mechanic and speaking directly to Tig.

Happy lit his cigar. 'I hope you like the taste of WD40 in your breakfast, young lady.'

Elijah waved his hands at the clouds of blue smoke wafting his way. 'Happy, do you really have to smoke that filthy thing so close to me?'

Grumbling, Happy walked away, puffing industriously at his cigar.

'Ignore him,' Wyatt said. 'Come on back to the garage with us.'

This was all happening so fast. Only a couple of hours ago, she had been splitting up with her boyfriend and now she had a bunch of new friends and a bed for the night.

They climbed into a gleaming minibus, Tig settling down next to Eve. Eve wondered where the luxury convertible was, but then she saw Wyatt climbing into the minibus driving seat.

'What about Happy?' she said.

'He never rides on the bus,' Wyatt said.

Eve was about to ask how he was going to get back when she heard the deep-throated roar of an engine. Happy zipped past on a motorbike, the cigar still clamped between his lips.

'There he goes, your friend and mine, Happy Hudson,' Elijah drawled.

Wyatt started up the engine.

Eve looked out of her window and wondered just what she was getting herself into.

Whatever it was, though, it was exciting.

4

Wyatt drove them out of the city centre and on to the autoroute. The minibus was air-conditioned, and the cool freshness of the interior was a relief from the heat outside.

'Is it always this hot in Monaco?' Eve asked.

'Not quite, no,' Tig replied. 'According to the weather guys, there's a storm on the way. We're just hoping it doesn't interfere with the Grand Prix schedule.'

It didn't take them long to arrive at their destination, an industrial complex of massive warehouses just off the autoroute and surrounded by pleasant woodland. Wyatt pulled the minibus to a stop by a massive, square building with a huge sign proclaiming it to be the home of Bailey-Kinsey MotorSports. A slogan beneath read,

SPEED, POWER, INNOVATION — FOR A BETTER FUTURE.

There were other units housing racing teams, but none as big or as grand as this one.

There was also a racing track, with sharp loops and corners and long straights.

Inside the workshop, Eve had expected it to be hot and noisy, but instead the cavernous space was clean and bright. Shelves and workspaces with engine parts, tyres, tools and computers with massive flat monitors lined the perimeter.

In the centre, raised from the floor on a hoist, sat a sleek, vibrantly coloured racing car. Eve stared, lost for a moment in its beauty.

'Quite something, isn't she?' Wyatt said, standing beside her.

'It's amazing,' Eve replied in hushed tones.

'She,' Wyatt corrected Eve. 'Annalise gets offended if you call her an it.'

Eve laughed. 'Annalise, I apologise, and I won't do it again.'

'We've been working on the design for

the last twenty years, first my father and now me.' Wyatt began walking around the car, obviously proud of its design and beauty. 'This car is going to revolution-ise professional racing the world over, dragging the sport into the twenty-first century with clean, carbon-neutral engines and sustainability at its heart.' He paused, and glanced back at Eve. 'Sorry, I went into salesman drive there.'

'That's OK, you're obviously so pas-sionate about this, I forgive you.'

Wyatt grinned. 'Thank you. Now, how many of these cars can I interest you in purchasing, Madam?'

Eve giggled. 'I'll take twenty. Have them delivered by tomorrow morning, please.'

'Excellent news, Madam. That will be one hundred and forty million pounds, then, please.'

Eve's jaw dropped open. 'What?'

Wyatt grinned again. 'It's a fantastic deal, right? Each one of these cars costs at least eight million, so you're getting a massive discount.'

Happy had arrived at the garage before the rest of the crew. He ambled over, scrubbing at his oil stained hands with a filthy rag.

'What kept you?' he said, his teeth clenching the extinguished stub of a cigar in one corner of his mouth. 'Did you take the scenic route, or did you stop for brunch?'

'Supposedly I'm in charge,' Wyatt said to Eve. 'But as you see, Happy is the real taskmaster around here.' He clapped his hands twice. 'Right, guys, let's get some work done. I want to take this beautiful lady out for a test drive before you lot start thinking about lunch. Let's go!'

Eve's heart leapt at Wyatt's description of her as a beautiful lady, although she was surprised at how forward he was being. And then she reddened as she realised he was referring to Annalise. Fortunately no one was looking her way, and Eve managed to hide her embarrassment.

She was amazed at Wyatt's transformation. Back at the cafe he had appeared laid back, but now he was striding up and down and barking orders at his crew. He was fully in charge, and Eve was sure he had forgotten all about her for the moment.

She hovered by the racing car, unsure of where she should put herself or what she should do. Her initial excitement began to fade as she suddenly felt like a spare part. She was scared to move in case she just put herself in the way of these people and their single-minded concentration.

As if sensing her discomfort, Wyatt appeared at her side and took her gently by the arm.

'Let's find you somewhere to relax. I'm sorry, this isn't going to be much fun for you for the next half an hour or so.'

'Oh no, I love it!'

Wyatt gave her a quizzical look. 'Seriously?'

'Yes, it's just ... so exciting! You said the AGP is an amateur race, but is this the sort of thing you do for a living?'

Wyatt chuckled. 'I suppose you could

say that.'

'Now I'm intrigued.' Eve allowed him to guide her through the workshop to a sofa and chairs grouped around a table. 'What does that mean?'

Wyatt gave her a smile. 'We'll talk later, all right? Let me know if you need anything.'

Eve watched Wyatt return to his crew of mechanics. Observing him walk away, she realised he had a certain swagger about him, a confidence. If racing wasn't his career, what else could it be? He had to be financing this somehow. Wyatt was being very mysterious, but Eve was determined to find out more.

Tig appeared with a mug of tea.

Eve laughed. 'Is this for me?'

'Compliments of the boss. I'll just leave it here.' Tig placed the mug on the table in front of Eve and gave her a thoughtful look. 'I think Wyatt has taken quite a shine to you.'

Eve's face grew warm with embarrassment.

'What? Of course he hasn't!'

Tig just smiled and walked away.

Now the excitement was replaced by a flustered feeling. *Wyatt has taken a shine to me?* But they had only just met! Butterflies fluttered in Eve's stomach. She had only just split up with Scott, she shouldn't even be thinking about another man just yet, but she had to admit, she thought she might have taken a shine to Wyatt too.

He was certainly cute; well, actually, a lot more than just cute, he was absolutely gorgeous. But she knew nothing about him. Not even what his job was, as he had been very mysterious about that. She had thought he was a mechanic, and then found out he was driving Annalise the racing car. But that still did not explain enough for Eve.

Her mind flashed back to when they first met, and his comment about how she should choose her boyfriends more carefully, and the argument they had. She'd been so cross at the time, but maybe they'd just got off on the wrong foot. He'd been so kind, and he really did seem to like her.

Eve suddenly realised her heart was racing. She concentrated on her breathing. It was a trick of hers to keep her anchored in the moment. Keep her centred when the world around her was off kilter. And it was certainly off kilter at the moment.

The breathing technique worked, and Eve began to relax.

Until the fat man stepped in front of her, blocking her view of the garage, almost blocking out the light.

'Well, young lady, you certainly have a ringside seat there, don't you?'

'I beg your pardon?'

Eve took an instant dislike to him. This was unusual, as she liked most people. That was something her friends sometimes told her off for; that she was far too trusting sometimes. But not this time. Whoever this man was, her instincts were on high alert.

The man reached up and pulled a hat off his head.

'No, I beg your pardon,' he said. 'The

name's Solomon Sisters, and I work for the Bailey-Kinseys. And you are?'

'Eve Parker.' She began to stand, but Sisters waved her back.

'Oh don't stand up on account of me.' He lowered his bulk onto the settee next to her. 'Now, it's hotter than a sauna in the Sahara in here, wouldn't you agree?'

Eve shifted, trying to keep as much distance between her and this strange man as she could. Her dislike for him was growing stronger. Was it because he had sat on the sofa next to her, instead of taking one of the chairs as most people would have done? He had invaded her personal space without a second thought, and his immense bulk made it even worse.

Sisters waved his hat in front of his face.

'So tell me, what's a pretty young lady like you doing here? You get lost on the way to the manicurist? Or are you here applying for a secretarial position? You don't look like a grease-monkey, that's for sure.'

'And I'm not sure I like your tone, Mr Sisters,' Eve said.

'Oh, I get told that a lot,' Sisters replied. 'Always poking my nose into other people's business, that's me. But I don't take no mind, you see, it's my job to ask questions. I'm what you might call a private investigator.'

'And you're here to investigate me?' Eve said.

Sisters chuckled and his huge belly wobbled. 'Well, not specifically, no, but you are currently a person of interest seeing as how you're sitting here watching Mr Bailey-Kinsey and his team working on their fandangled new electric motor, in which there has been tremendous interest from other parties.'

'You think I'm a spy?'

Sisters leaned in towards her, and Eve caught a whiff of body odour. 'Are you?'

'Of course not!'

Much to Eve's relief, Sisters sat back again. 'Well now, that's all right then.' He scratched his head in a display of mock puzzlement. 'Except, if you are a spy, then of course you're going to deny it. Am I right, Miss Parker?'

'You're teasing me,' Eve said.

Sisters chuckled again. 'Uh-huh, I suppose I am at that. I know you're no spy, you're just another one in the endless line of girls our young Mr Bailey-Kinsey over there enjoys parading around town.'

'An endless line?' Eve said, a sudden rush of jealousy getting the better of her.

Sisters nodded. 'Oh yes indeed. Don't you know who you're dating, Miss Parker? That there is Mr Wyatt Bailey-Kinsey, millionaire philanthropist, racing driver, and all round playboy.'

Eve swallowed. A millionaire?

Sisters chuckled again, his belly wobbling.

'You had no idea, had you?' He leaned in close again. 'Don't get your hopes up, young lady. Wyatt gets bored pretty easy like, and before you know it, he'll have moved on to the next girl and you'll be left behind, your head spinning, asking yourself just what the heck happened there.'

Eve swallowed again. All of a sudden, her surroundings seemed to be closing in on her, and sucking out all the air. She stood up abruptly.

'I have to go.'

Eve walked away, stiff-legged and awkward from all the tension in her muscles. Behind her, she could hear Sisters laughing again. She stepped outside and took a deep breath of fresh air. An engine roared into life and a long, sleek racing car appeared from one of the other units. It drove onto the track and then, with a sudden roar and squeal of tyres, it sped away.

Eve watched it as it took the bends easily, driving at speeds she could hardly imagine.

'Exciting, isn't it?'

Eve jumped at the voice. Wyatt was beside her at the wheel of the racing car. Somehow, he had driven up beside her without making a noise.

Wyatt laughed. 'Sorry, I didn't mean to surprise you.'

'Your car, it's so quiet.'

'One of the features of electric engines; very little noise.'

'Are you going to race it?'

'No, just taking it for a test drive on the track.'

Happy appeared, chewing on a fresh, unlit cigar. 'Don't push her too hard, those bearings need a little settling time.' The cigar moved from one side of his mouth to the other as he talked.

Wyatt saluted. 'Yes, sir!'

With a wave and a grin, Wyatt eased the long, sleek car onto the track. Suddenly, with barely a whisper from the engine, he pushed the speed up, and the car seemed to take off, almost flying.

Happy shook his head.

'I told him not to do that.'

'Does he ever listen to anyone else?' Eve said.

Happy regarded Eve thoughtfully for a second.

'You catch on quick, don't you?' He glanced over his shoulder, back at the car workshop. 'Piece of advice for you. That slimeball, Sisters? Stay away from him.'

Happy turned his head to gaze out at the track and watch Wyatt pushing the car's speed up as it tore around the track. Eve was tempted to ask him what he meant about Sisters, but she had the feeling Happy wasn't going to be drawn into any more conversation.

Instead, she watched Wyatt. He was amazing. She could hardly believe that he could control a car at such frightening speeds, but he did. He took the sharp bends with ease, barely slowing down, or so it seemed, and not once going into a skid or losing control. Surely he would have no problem winning the Monaco Grand Prix?

The previous driver who had taken his car out pulled into his pit stop. His mechanics were watching Wyatt's progress around the track. He was entering the final bend.

Happy murmured, 'This is going to be his fastest time on this track.' He glanced at Eve. 'You probably don't realise how big a deal this is, but if Wyatt wins the

Grand Prix tomorrow, he's showing the world that electric engines can compete against fossil fuel powered engines for both speed and power.'

'So it's not just personal ambition for Wyatt?' Eve said, surprised that Happy was talking to her.

'Nope.' Happy chewed on his cigar. 'We win tomorrow, we'll have investors fighting each other to throw money at us. Renewable electricity is the future of motor sports, but the old fossils in charge of the fossil fuel industry need to realise that. And they will, after to —'

Happy stopped talking and his mouth hung open, the cigar dropping from it.

Suddenly Wyatt's racing car had spun out of control. Before Eve could react, it flipped over. A side panel split off and bounced across the track. The car continued to roll, flipping over again with a crunch of metal and plastic. Finally, it came to rest upside down. Black smoke poured from the engine. A tyre rolled towards them, yellow flames just visible in the brightness of the day flowering along the black rubber tread.

A silence and a stillness enveloped Eve, as though she were trapped in a microcosm of time. She was frozen in this moment, like a snapshot of the scene as it happened.

And then the moment broke. Happy took off at a surprisingly speedy run towards the car, followed by Elijah and Tig. Crew members from other teams ran to provide help too.

Eve joined them. She pelted across the track, one thought in her mind: *Don't be dead! Please!*

As she approached the wrecked car, she slowed down. Smoke billowed up in a dark, ominous cloud. The ground was littered with shattered pieces of glass and plastic. Eve's hands flew to her mouth when she saw the growing pool of dark liquid on the track beneath the upturned car.

The panic was swiftly followed by relief when she realised she was looking at oil, not blood.

Eve held back, knowing she would

just be in the way if she tried to help. Wyatt's car was surrounded by a small crowd now, and it seemed to Eve they all knew exactly what to do, as though they rehearsed regularly for situations like this.

Tig blasted a small fire extinguisher at the chassis. Eve couldn't see any flames now, but smoke still poured out. Happy and Elijah were on hands and knees, peering beneath the car. Happy reached out. Eve gasped as she saw Wyatt's hand appear and grab hold of Happy's.

With the help of other teams, Elijah pushed at the car, levering it up enough that Happy was able to drag Wyatt out from beneath the wreck.

An ambulance raced onto the track, and a paramedic jumped out. From what Eve could see, Wyatt seemed to be all right. Then she lost sight of him as his rescuers crowded around him.

★ ★ ★

The tall woman with the bird-like nose and an air of perpetual disappointment about her looked Eve up and down and sniffed.

'Well, come on! Don't just sit there staring at me like a startled rabbit. What do you have to say for yourself?'

'I . . . um . . . I . . .'

'Goodness me, but you are a timid little thing, aren't you? Where does he find them, I ask myself? Where on earth does he find them?'

'Hello Mrs B,' Tig said, appearing beside Eve like a rescuing angel. 'Wyatt is just being checked over by a doctor, but they've said he should be fine to go home today.'

Mrs Bailey-Kinsey regarded Tig with barely any less disdain than she had Eve.

'You're one of the mechanics, aren't you? The one with the funny name.'

'Tig, Mrs B, my name is Tig.'

The accident and emergency waiting area was crowded, hot and stuffy. A child started crying and Eve knew just how they felt. She wasn't entirely sure how she had ended up at the hospital with Tig, everything had happened so fast.

And then Mrs Penelope Bailey-Kinsey had arrived, Wyatt's stepmother. Her sharp voice went perfectly with her sharp-featured face. Her fingers, ears and neck dripped with jewellery, and the sleek dress she wore looked more suited to an evening meal than a visit to the hospital.

'You, I say, you,' she called out to a passing medic, waving at him like he was a waiter in a restaurant. 'My stepson, where is he? How long are you people going to fuss over him for? Goodness me, we've been here for hours.'

'If you'd like to take a seat, I'm sure someone will be out soon with more news,' the medic said and hurried away before Mrs Bailey-Kinsey could reply. She snorted at his retreating back.

'Why on earth did you allow him to be brought here?' She returned her stern gaze to Tig. 'He knows perfectly well that we have private medical insurance.'

'I think because it was an emergency,

Mrs B,' Tig said.

Mrs Bailey-Kinsey regarded the waiting room with an undisguised expression of disgust.

'Well, I'm not spending any more time waiting here. Who knows what I might catch? Wyatt can telephone me when he's finished being prodded and poked.'

She turned to go, but stopped as she heard her name being called.

'Penelope!'

Eve saw Wyatt walking into the waiting room. He was still wearing his racing overalls, smudged with oil stains. A nasty bruise had sprung out on his forehead, but otherwise he looked fine.

Wyatt and his stepmother stood facing each other as if an invisible barrier separated them. Eve wasn't surprised that Mrs Bailey-Kinsey made no move to give her stepson a hug, or show him any kind of affection.

'Honestly, how many times have I told you not to race with those experimental engines of yours? They'll be the death of you yet, just like your father!'

Wyatt suddenly glowered at Penelope, and he opened his mouth to speak.

'What did the doctor say?' Tig said, jumping in before Wyatt could reply.

'That he needs to rest,' the doctor said, appearing beside Wyatt. He wore a shirt and a spotted bow tie, with his shirt sleeves rolled up.

Wyatt turned to face the others. 'I've got a mild concussion, but otherwise I'm fine,' he said, and paused. 'I might have to stay in overnight though.'

'Oh no, why?' Eve said.

Mrs Bailey-Kinsey gave her a swift, sharp glance, as though to reprimand her for speaking out of turn.

Wyatt gave Eve a weary smile. 'I was knocked out in the accident, I think I was unconscious for no more than a few seconds, but the doctor says I'm at risk of a bleed on the brain.'

'He needs someone with him for the next twenty-four hours, just to keep an eye on him,' the consultant said. 'He has to stay awake for the next twelve hours at least, as the dangers of a sub-cerebral haemorrhage are a distinct possibility.' He gave Wyatt a hard stare. 'I have strongly insisted that Wyatt remain with us in hospital overnight so that we can keep a close eye on him, but he insists on discharging himself.'

Mrs Bailey-Kinsey tutted and scowled at Wyatt.

'Just like your father, such an obstinate boy.'

'I've also strongly advised him against racing in the Grand Prix.'

'Oh no, seriously?' Tig said.

'Seriously.' The consultant looked grave. 'He may appear fine and healthy right now, but in the next twenty-four hours, a lot could change. Now, who is going to volunteer to look after this young man, or do I have to insist he remains with us under our medical supervision?'

Mrs Bailey-Kinsey sniffed and turned away, as though discovering something fascinating to look at on the other side of the waiting area. An uncomfortable silence stretched out.

'Maybe I should come and stay with

you,' Eve said, and then blushed at her sudden boldness. 'I trained as a nurse and then decided to take six months out to travel.'

'Excellent!' the consultant said. 'Things to be aware of are any fainting spells, sleepiness, sudden headaches or uncharacteristic changes in mood.'

Eve nodded.

Wyatt grinned. 'That sounds perfect, my own nurse to take care of me.'

'Just until tomorrow, obviously,' Eve said. She turned to Tig. 'Sorry I'm not bunking with you at the garage after all.'

'That's probably wise,' Tig said. 'That comment Happy made about WD40 is kind of true.'

'Well, that's settled,' Mrs Bailey-Kinsey said, turning her attention back to Wyatt. 'Now darling, don't forget, you're attending the Mayor's ball tonight. I hope you've found someone more suitable than that little floozy you dragged along last time, she looked like something the cat brought in.' She gave Eve, a swift up-and-down look. 'You might do,

I suppose. I can't imagine you have anything to wear though, do you?'

Before Eve could answer, Mrs Bailey-Kinsey turned on her heel and walked towards the exit, her head held high as though seeking fresh air and an escape from the stink of common humanity.

Eve was speechless. She felt as if she had been placed under a microscope and examined like a lab experiment gone wrong.

'Ignore her,' Wyatt said, turning to Eve and Tig. 'And hey, thank you.'

'That's OK,' Eve said, watching Penelope until she disappeared through the sliding doors.

'Let me give you guys a lift,' Tig said, flashing a brief smile at Eve. 'It's been a long day.'

5

'Looks like you're stuck with me now,' Wyatt said, as they stood on the roof terrace situated high above Monte Carlo, overlooking the apartment buildings, the winding streets, and the ocean.

'This is all yours?' Eve gasped, hardly able to believe what her eyes were telling her. 'I can't believe you live here, this is amazing!'

'Well, I don't actually live here — not all the time anyway,' Wyatt replied. 'This is my holiday home.'

'This is your holiday home?'

'One of my holiday homes, actually.'

'One of your holiday homes?'

'You do realise you're repeating everything I'm saying, don't you?'

'I'm repeating everything . . . ? Oh. Sorry.' Eve tore her gaze away from the Monte Carlo skyline and the view of the ocean beyond it. She remembered now,

77

that unpleasant private eye with the strange name, Solomon Sisters, telling her that Wyatt was a millionaire playboy. In all the excitement of the crash, she had forgotten.

'I just . . . I don't . . . I can't believe it. How rich are you?'

'Personally, or the whole family?'

'But, you never said anything, nobody told me.'

'What did you expect? Hi, my name's Wyatt and I'm on the Sunday Times Rich List?'

'You're on the Sunday Times Rich List?'

'In the top ten, actually.'

'In the top ten?'

'There you go again, repeating everything.'

'I think I need to catch my breath.'

'Would you like to sit down?' Wyatt suggested.

'No, I'm OK,' Eve replied, and then promptly sat down on a cushioned wicker chair, next to the jacuzzi and only a few feet away from the infinity swimming pool.

Wyatt sat beside her looking concerned.

'It's all right, I just need a second,' Eve said. 'It's just, this morning I split up with my boyfriend and I was homeless and penniless, and now here I am about to spend the night in a millionaire's holiday mansion.'

'Um, billionaire actually.'

Eve dropped her head into her hands and began laughing. 'Of course, how silly of me!'

'Do you need to lie down for a moment? I'm starting to worry about you.'

Eve raised a hand. 'No, I'll be fine, I just need a moment.'

'What about a stiff drink? Brandy? Whisky? Perhaps something stronger? Smelling salts?'

Eve lifted her head to see Wyatt grinning at her.

'Stop teasing me!'

'I can't help it.' Wyatt chuckled. 'The look on your face is priceless! You are so easy to tease.'

'Is this how you treat all the girls you bring up here?' Eve said.

'Who says I've brought any girls up here before you?' Wyatt replied.

Eve thought of Solomon Sisters, and what he'd said about Wyatt and the endless line of girls he enjoyed parading around town. About how Wyatt would have moved onto the next girl before Eve knew what was happening.

'Well, you're a billionaire, aren't you?'

Wyatt raised an eyebrow. 'And your point is?'

You must have a different girl on your arm every night, she wanted to say. *You've probably brought hundreds of girls up to your penthouse. And I'm just the latest in a very long line.*

'Oh, nothing.'

'Nothing?' Wyatt laughed. 'Sure, I believe that. I know what you're thinking.'

Eve arched an eyebrow. 'Oh do you, now?'

'You're thinking, *I bet he has a different girl on his arm every night, and he's proba-*

bly brought hundreds of girls up here before now, and I'm just the latest in an endless line of them.'

Eve reddened a little. That was almost word perfect. What was he, psychic or something?

'I'm right, aren't I?' Wyatt said, teasing.

'No, actually,' Eve replied, turning her head to look out across Monte Carlo.

This was silly. Why didn't she just ask him: *Do you have a different girl on your arm every night?*

She turned back to look at Wyatt, resolving to be honest with him and ask the question.

But before the words were formed and ready to speak out loud, Wyatt stood up. He grabbed Eve by the hand and hauled her to her feet.

'Come on, let me show you around. Did you bring your swimming costume? You might have noticed the pool.'

Eve buried her doubts about Wyatt. She was going to spend one night here, to make sure he suffered no ill effects from his bump on the head. Tomorrow she would call her parents and book a flight home.

They walked down a short flight of steps. They were so high, Eve had a moment of giddy dizziness. The infinity pool jutted out over the edge of the penthouse terrace, its water so still and clear it was like a mirror, and reflected the blue sky above. In the distance, Eve saw the buildings squashed together that made up Monte Carlo, and the hills behind the city. Wyatt's holiday home was situated in the Les Moneghetti district, which had survived the modernisation of the rest of Monte Carlo. Here the streets snaked between traditional buildings and homes, sometimes along the edge of a cliff face. Somehow though, from this distance, the old and new parts of the district all looked beautiful and magical once more — the Monte Carlo of Hollywood films and legend.

'This is amazing,' Eve whispered.

'It is that,' Wyatt said. 'And believe me, I do realise how lucky I am, but the view isn't why I am here. I've already sunk a huge amount of money into funding this new electric engine, and if I win the AGP tomorrow, we will get more investment into developing the technology further. Eve, I'm looking to transform more than just the racing world, I'm working to bring sustainability and green power to the world at large.' He paused. 'Sorry, I've gone into sales talk mode again.'

'No apologies needed,' Eve said. 'What you're doing sounds amazing.'

'Enough of the shop talk! Let me grab a shower and then we can relax in the pool with a drink. Seriously, did you bring a swimming costume?'

'Uh, yes, I did,' Eve replied, thinking of her faded bikini which, before leaving Britain for her adventure with Scott, she'd decided had one more summer left in it.

'Great. Come on, I'll show you to your room.'

★ ★ ★

Floating in the pool with a drink in her hand, Eve began to feel the tension of the last few hours draining away. This was utter heaven. She gazed up at the clear blue sky. Hadn't someone mentioned earlier that there was a storm on the way? Right now, she couldn't believe it.

She sighed contentedly, finding it hard to believe that hours earlier she had been on the street far down below, hot and sweaty, arguing with her now ex-boyfriend. Now look at her!

After showing her to a guest room, one of how many more Eve didn't know, Wyatt had left her to freshen up and change into her bikini. He had also provided her with a silky, cool dressing gown, perhaps mindful of the fact that they had only met earlier that day and she might be a little shy.

The guest bedroom alone was larger than Eve's living room back in England, and the bed itself was so massive she feared she might get lost in it. But it was the view that took her breath away every single time. That unimaginable vista; the sky, the sea, and Monte Carlo.

Was she dreaming? Any minute now would she come back to reality and realise she was still standing on the harbour front, arguing with Scott?

Eve pushed the thought away.

When she came back down to the terrace and the pool, she found Wyatt had left out drinks and towels by the sun loungers. Or did he have a butler or a maid to do that? Eve hadn't seen anyone else since she arrived, but she couldn't be sure her and Wyatt were alone here.

She was grateful to have arrived at the pool before him, as it meant she could slip into the water where her faded bikini might be less obvious. If she'd known she was going to meet a billionaire and go for a dip in his pool, she would definitely have bought a new one. She just hoped he wouldn't notice how old it was, or even worse, pass a comment on it.

The infinity pool was blissfully cool enough to be refreshing. She swam to the edge and looked out over the white city, and the blue ocean and the yachts in the harbour, all shimmering in the late afternoon sunlight. What a bizarre turn of events. Eve smiled as she imagined Scott's reaction if he could see her now.

Thinking of Scott turned Eve's mood a little darker. She wondered what he was doing and if he had found anywhere to stay for the night. Perhaps she should text him, to check he was OK. After all, it hadn't just been Eve who had no money left.

Unless of course he'd lied about that too.

Then again, he might well have gone crawling back to that maid he had a fling with. The two of them deserved each other.

Here Eve was, floating in a pool in a billionaire's holiday home, and all she could think of was her weaselly ex-boyfriend. She just needed to forget him, then she could relax and enjoy herself. But the more she tried not to think of Scott, the more she couldn't get him out of her head.

A tiny flutter of discomfort and nerves blossomed into life in Eve's stomach. It seemed that every man she had dated, although there weren't that many, to be honest, had been a lying cheat. Somehow, she just seemed to gravitate towards them.

And she couldn't help but think, what if it had happened again? After all, she knew very little about Wyatt Bailey-Kinsey. Up until an hour ago, she hadn't even known he was a millionaire — sorry, billionaire. And now here she was, floating in his swimming pool with a drink in her hand, waiting for him to join her.

And then what? He had been a perfect gentleman so far, but now he had her alone in his penthouse suite. Could she trust him? Was the gentlemanly appearance nothing more than an act? A way of luring prospective dates up to his penthouse?

What had she been thinking? He wasn't her boyfriend. She shouldn't even be considering another relationship after splitting with Scott only hours ago. It didn't seem right.

Eve straightened herself out and her feet touched the pool's floor. She placed her glass on the edge.

Maybe I should leave, she thought. *This is silly, what did I think I was doing, volunteering to stay the night with him?*

But wait, you agreed to stay because of his accident. The doctor said he needs someone with him for twelve hours to make sure he doesn't suffer from an accidental bleed on the brain.

The tiny flutter of nerves in Eve's stomach suddenly erupted into a mass of panicked butterflies as she realised she hadn't seen Wyatt for at least fifteen minutes. What if he had collapsed in his bedroom, or in the shower? Here she was in the pool, sipping on a drink and enjoying the view when he could be lying unconscious, or even worse dead, in his bathroom.

Eve swam towards the pool's edge. All her doubts about his character, and her possible lack of safety, had disappeared. She needed to get out of the water and check that he was all right. Placing her hands on the side, she pushed herself out of the water. Dripping wet, she ran barefoot across the patio, leaving dark footprints. She didn't even think about the dressing gown.

Wyatt stepped out of the apartment, wearing swim shorts, a towel draped over his shoulder.

'Oh, hello,' he said.

Eve screamed, turned and ran back to the pool, where she jumped into the water.

Wyatt started laughing.

'Do I look that hideous in swim shorts?'

'No,' Eve said, blinking water out of her eyes and spluttering. 'You surprised me!'

Feeling her cheeks warm with embarrassment, Eve slipped completely beneath the water. She propelled herself to the bottom, where she sat cross-legged on the floor for a moment. It was quiet and peaceful down here. Patterns of light played along the pool floor and sides, becoming almost hypnotic in the shifting patterns.

Knowing she couldn't stay down here forever, Eve pushed against the floor with her feet and glided up and back to the surface.

Wyatt had settled into a sun lounger and was sipping at a drink.

'You know, you really are the strangest nurse I have ever met. Was this part of your training?'

'Stop teasing me!' Eve exclaimed, but smiled despite herself. 'This is all so very strange and new to me. I've never stayed with a millionaire, sorry I mean billionaire playboy before.'

Wyatt looked at her.

'What makes you think I'm a playboy?'

'Aren't all billionaires playboys?' she retorted.

'No, we're not. In fact, we are a vastly misunderstood section of society.'

Eve couldn't help but smile.

'Oh, that's terrible. It must be so hard on you having all that money and no one understanding what a terrible burden it is.'

'Now you're teasing me!'

Wyatt stood up. His taut, muscular physique took Eve's breath away for a second.

Then he ran to the edge of the pool and threw himself in, wrapping his body up into a tight ball. Water splashed everywhere, all over the patio and over Eve. Coughing and laughing, she backed away as he surfaced and shook his head like a dog, his long hair spraying even more water.

'Stop it!' she screamed, but still laughing.

'After teasing me like that? No way!' Wyatt began advancing upon her.

Eve backed up, laughing. 'Oh no, what are you doing? Stay away, all right? Stay away!'

Wyatt didn't stay away.

6

Solomon Sisters was a man who took great delight in his profession. What was it Mark Twain had said? *Find a job you love and you will never work a day in your life*. That was it. Sisters had heard that somewhere, not that he could remember where now.

That Mark Twain, he must have been a clever fella. But then Sisters had tried reading one of his books once, which one was it now? Oh yes, *Huckleberry Finn*. He hadn't got more than a few pages into it before he'd discarded it, bored and disappointed. To be fair, Sisters wasn't a big reader, but he'd expected something more than what he got.

But yes, Sisters enjoyed being a private investigator, and none of what he did felt like work to him. He took great pleasure in every aspect of his day-to-day routine. Like his job tonight, trying to find someone.

It would be easy to get lost in Monte Carlo, especially when the Monaco Alternative Grand Prix was gearing up to be full on in the next couple of days. The city was never busier, every hotel, bed-and-breakfast, youth hostel, spare room and sofa fully booked up. At no other point in the year were so many people crammed into the city. But Sisters was never one to be put off by a challenge.

It helped that his quarry most likely didn't have any money. When she broke up with her boyfriend, Eve was broke, which meant Scott Saunders was probably penniless too. In which case, he was in trouble and would be looking for charity.

That made it easier to find him.

Sisters knew his reputation, he knew that generally people didn't much like him, which made it difficult at times to foster someone's confidence, and encourage them to confide in him. But he was a good eavesdropper.

Hanging around at the garage long enough and listening in to Tig and Elijah gossiping had got him all the information he needed about Miss Eveline Parker. When he had heard about Scott, Sisters had seen a way in, of getting what he wanted.

And what his employer needed.

Sisters hitched up his trousers and adjusted his hat. It was likely going to be a long afternoon of pounding the streets, going from hotel to hotel until he found Scott Saunders.

Sisters didn't mind. It was all part of the job.

A job that he enjoyed so very much.

★ ★ ★

'Oh my gosh, just look at her!' Eve exclaimed, giggling.

'It's hard to believe, isn't it?' Wyatt said.

As the sun had slowly set and the evening drawn in, Eve and Wyatt had dried off and gone indoors. Wyatt cooked them a meal, something he said was thrown together from leftovers in the fridge, but turned out to be an absolutely delicious concoction of Mediterranean vegetables, chicken, and a sweet, sticky sauce.

Wyatt poured them both a glass of white wine, cold and crisp and sparkling on the tongue. Eve had protested that Wyatt should not be drinking after having bumped his head and lost consciousness, but he told her he would be fine.

Eve didn't argue. She was getting the feeling that Wyatt was used to having his own way, and that he didn't take advice or instruction from anyone. Was that typical of billionaire playboys? she wondered.

After the meal, they had settled down in what Wyatt referred to as 'The Cinema'. This was a cavernous room, possibly taking up an entire floor of the penthouse, with one long sofa filled with cushions in the middle of it. On a wall was a screen and from the opposite wall shone the light of a projector.

'What are we going to watch?' Eve had

asked.

'Wait and see,' Wyatt had replied, a mischievous look playing across his face.

The film started up and Wyatt settled down on the sofa next to Eve, but with space between them. She was grateful; she had been a little nervous that he might try to cuddle up to her, especially after their high jinx in the pool. Instead, he gave her space, and Eve respected that.

The movie was a colourful 1960s romantic comedy, involving a handsome leading man who looked vaguely familiar, playing against type as a socially awkward scientist, and a young actress called Dusty Day playing a wacky, dizzy blonde with whom he falls in love. The offbeat comedy delivered jokes thick and fast, and Eve found herself laughing out loud along with Wyatt.

After the first twenty minutes, Eve had turned to Wyatt and said, 'This is good fun and everything, but why exactly are you showing this to me?'

Wyatt had chuckled.

'Take another look. Doesn't Dusty Day look even slightly familiar to you?'

Eve looked again at the beautiful young woman on the screen.

'I don't know — maybe she looks a little familiar but I can't place her.'

'Maybe it would help if I told you that you met her earlier today.'

Eve had gasped, throwing a hand over her mouth. 'No! Is that Penelope?'

Wyatt laughed. 'Quite the beauty in her day, wasn't she?'

'And now she's . . .' Eve faltered, suddenly realising that she was in danger of insulting Wyatt's stepmother, '. . . so elegant.'

'Oh come on, that wasn't what you were going to say!' Wyatt exclaimed, laughing even harder.

'Well . . .'

'Be honest, what you're really thinking is, *and now she's such a bitter, twisted and unpleasant woman who looks down on everyone she meets as though we are lesser mortals and just a little bit smelly.* Right?'

'I wouldn't have gone that far,' Eve

said.

'Then you wouldn't have gone far enough,' Wyatt said, his laughter subsiding. 'She's my stepmother, but that doesn't mean to say I like her. And the feeling's mutual. I'm amazed she turned up at the hospital today when she got news of my crash. Maybe she suspected there might be a news crew outside, she's always on the lookout for some free publicity in the hope that she can restart her stalled movie career.'

Wyatt picked up the remote and hit the pause button. Dusty Day froze in mid laughter, filling the screen with her beauty and vitality. In contrast, Wyatt's mood suddenly seemed to have grown darker.

'What happened?' Eve said, after a moment or two of silence.

'Hmm?' Wyatt stirred, almost as though he was waking from a slumber.

'To your mother and father? Where are they?'

'My mother died shortly after I was born. She had an infection, and that turned into sepsis and then she was gone. My dad met Penelope when I was six or seven, I think, and they married after a whirlwind romance.' He laughed, a sharp, bitter bark. 'You know the saying *marry in haste, repent at leisure*. I think my dad identified with that.'

'Did they divorce?'

Wyatt ran a hand through his tousled hair.

'No, my dad died in a car crash when I was ten. He was a racing driver, at the top of his game. But he was an inventor too, and he'd been developing a new, much more efficient petrol engine when the crash happened.'

Like father, like son, Eve thought.

'Did he crash during a race?' she asked.

Wyatt nodded. 'Yeah, the Monte Carlo Grand Prix. My father and Calvino Ruggiero's father were the favourites to win. There had been a bitter rivalry between them for years, and the Grand Prix was almost a grudge match between them, it was as if none of the other competitors mattered.'

'I guess the race was halted when your father's car crashed, right?'

'Only while the wreckage was hauled off the track and my father pulled out. Once the route was clear again, the race continued, and Italo Ruggiero was crowned the winner.'

Eve sat up straighter.

'But that's awful. How could they continue the race when your father had died in the crash?'

'He died later that day.' A shadow seemed to have fallen over Wyatt's face as he relived the past. 'The crew pulled him out of his car and he was checked over by medics and he seemed absolutely fine.' Wyatt paused. 'He died later that night of an acute brain haemorrhage.'

A chill swept through Eve. Wasn't this exactly what the doctor was worried about with Wyatt? Couldn't he see the parallels of the story he was telling her and what had happened today?

'So, I lost my father and Italo Ruggiero won the Grand Prix. You'd have thought that would be the end of the two families' rivalry, wouldn't you? But no, Calvino is stoking it up again and now here we are, the next generation of billionaire playboy racing drivers competing against each other in the Grand Prix.'

'What about Italo, what happened to him?' Eve said.

'Oh, he's still around, although he doesn't race any more. In fact, I spotted his yacht out in the harbour earlier today. He'll be here to cheer his son on. Anyway, after Dad died, I inherited everything, his estate, his businesses, his personal wealth. Penelope got nothing, he'd written her out of the will entirely.'

'Oh, wow. That must have been hard for her.'

'Yeah, she didn't take it well. But by law she was my legal guardian, and so she stayed.'

'That was good of her, right?'

'Not really. By staying, she still had an income to fund her lavish lifestyle. And she took the lifestyle part seriously too, leaving me to be taken care of by a stream of nannies and personal tutors. I

101

hardly ever saw Penelope, but then that was how I preferred it.'

Eve looked at the screen, at the frozen image of the beautiful Dusty Day — her Sixties bob, her miniskirt and colourful top, her mouth open in laughter, showing off her perfect teeth and lips. For someone so beautiful, she had made Wyatt very miserable.

The thought of Wyatt losing his mother before he even knew her, and then losing his father at such a tender age, saddened Eve. Penelope, or Dusty Day, should have been there to care for him and lavish him with love.

Instead, she had turned her back on him. It was amazing to Eve that Wyatt had grown up into such a lovely, mature adult, whereas Penelope had grown twisted and bitter.

Eve gazed at Wyatt. His eyes looked unfocused and blank, as though inside his head he was somewhere else.

He's in the past, she thought. *A painful and terribly sad part of his life. I've got to do something here. He just looks so unhappy.*

Eve snatched the remote out of Wyatt's hand and turned the projector off. Dusty Day disappeared into a blank screen.

'That's enough of Dusty Day. It was a terrible movie, anyway. What shall we do now?'

'I don't know, what do you want to do?' Wyatt yawned.

'Oh no, that's not allowed, remember?' Eve said, jumping to her feet and grabbing Wyatt by the hand. 'Take me for a walk, show me around.'

Wyatt allowed himself to be hauled to his feet and, snapping out of his dark mood, grinned.

'I've got a better idea.'

'Come on, spill, what is it?' Eve said.

'It's a surprise,' Wyatt said. 'But you're going to love it!'

'Oh no, I'm not sure I like the sound of this,' Eve replied. 'Please, tell me what it is.'

Wyatt shook his head. 'Uh-uh, you're just going to have to wait. Come on.'

He held out his hand, and Eve took it.

As he led her out of his penthouse,

Eve didn't know if she was excited or nervous.

Actually, she did know. She was both.

7

Despite her protestations, Wyatt drove. Eve had told him he really shouldn't be putting himself in situations where he might be at risk, such as behind the wheel of a car, but he dismissed her concerns with a casual wave of his hand.

Wyatt Bailey-Kinsey obviously did not like taking instruction or advice from anyone.

At least his mood had lifted. He seemed alive once more, like the man she had met earlier.

He drove them down the winding road, clinging to the side of the hill on which the Les Moneghetti district was located. In the open-top car, Eve felt a sense of vertigo as she looked down at the steep, rocky drop. She wondered if there had ever been any accidents here, and she could imagine a car tumbling down the sheer drop, bursting into flames like a scene in a movie.

But she had no worries about that happening with Wyatt driving. He took the sharp bends in the road expertly and smoothly.

Well, that makes sense, she thought. *He is a racing driver, after all.*

He drove them back into Monte Carlo. It was early evening, but construction of the stands and the barriers for the Grand Prix was still under way.

'They'll work through the night,' Wyatt said. 'That way they can minimise disruption to the normal traffic flow by keeping the preparations for the event down to the minimum number of days.'

Wyatt took them out of the city centre and back to his garage, where floodlights had been switched on around the track and the workspace, despite the sun not having set yet. Eve heard the sound of machinery and music.

'Are they still working?' Eve said.

'They are, and I should be too,' Wyatt replied, climbing out of the car.

'But you're under doctor's orders to rest!' Eve cried out as she climbed out of the car and followed him.

Seriously? He thought this was a better idea than a quiet walk around his holiday home and the Les Moneghetti District? Coming back here to work on his car when he should be resting?

Eve resisted the urge to scream with frustration as she followed Wyatt into the garage. He was kind, generous and cute, but in the few hours Eve had known him, Wyatt seemed to be showing a more arrogant, hard-edged side to his personality. Especially now. Whenever she contradicted him, suggesting it wasn't a good idea that he drove, that returning to the garage to work wasn't the doctor's idea of resting, he simply waved her concerns away.

Again, Eve wondered if she had been a bad judge of character and that Wyatt wasn't suitable boyfriend material after all.

Wait a minute, she thought, *is this how you are thinking of him? Boyfriend material?*

Maybe.

But was she making a foolish choice again?

Eve's thoughts turned back to Scott. The contrast between the two men couldn't have been more pronounced, and Eve once again found herself wondering just what she had seen in Scott. She had to have seen something attractive in him, surely?

Yes, she remembered those first few weeks of their relationship, Scott had been funny and charming, but then over the following months he had gradually changed. It had happened so slowly at first that Eve hadn't noticed, as he grew more controlling, more needy, and increasingly selfish.

Something similar seemed to be happening with Wyatt, except his changes in mood were much more erratic and happening a lot faster. It had to be the concussion.

It had to be.

Inside the garage, Happy looked up as Wyatt entered, Eve trotting behind him.

'Here he is,' Happy grunted, an unlit

cigar clamped between his teeth. 'I told you he wouldn't be able to stay away.'

Elijah and Tig looked up from their work.

'Aren't you supposed to be resting, Boss?' Elijah drawled, wiping his hands on an oily rag.

Wyatt's racing car was up on an elevated stand and Tig was in the pit beneath it, her hands up in the car's insides.

'That's exactly what I'm doing,' Wyatt said, walking past the mechanics and up to Happy.

Eve rolled her eyes as she followed Wyatt. Tig saw her and burst into silent laughter.

'Have you found out what the problem is yet?' Wyatt asked.

Happy chewed on his cigar for a moment. 'Yeah, but you're not going to like it.'

'Tell me.'

Happy grabbed a flashlight from a bench and joined Tig under the car. Wyatt followed him.

'Right there,' Happy said, pointing

with the flashlight. 'You see that?'

Tig got out of the way and stood by Eve.

Eve gave her a brief smile, but she was too distracted to make conversation. Wyatt's mood seemed to have shifted and become much darker again. Was it watching that Dusty Day film that had brought him low? Or was it the sudden shifts in mood that the consultant warned them about?

Eve was beginning to regret offering to look after Wyatt. He was far too independent and obstinate to take any instruction or advice from her. And did she really have the knowledge or the skills to be aware of any signs of concussion?

Something in Happy's tone brought her faculties to attention. Even by Happy's standards, he sounded very unhappy. She edged a little closer, hoping to catch what they were saying.

'And you think it's sabotage?' Wyatt said.

'Uh-huh,' Happy grunted.

'How sure of that can you be?' Wyatt

persisted.

'About as sure as I am that you could have lost your life out there earlier — and that someone engineered it that way.'

Wyatt ran a hand through his tousled hair.

'But who would do something like that?'

Eve flinched as a booming voice ricocheted around the garage, cutting through her thoughts.

'Ah! He lives! He cheated death on the track once, but can he do it again on race day?'

Wyatt and Happy both straightened up and turned to face the newcomer.

'I guess you've come here just to gloat, haven't you?' Wyatt said.

The Italian bowed low with a smile.

'Why, of course. Continue like this, Mr Bailey-Kinsey, and you will not even reach the starting line, never mind the finish.'

He noticed Eve, and his smile grew even wider.

'But you have not introduced me to

your friend.' He sauntered up to Eve. 'I am Calvino Ruggiero, the greatest racing driver in the world.'

Eve stretched out a hand for him to shake, but he took it and bent down to give it a kiss. Happy snorted with laughter. Eve's face grew pink.

'Very pleased to meet you,' she said, although that wasn't how she felt at all. 'My name is Eve.'

'Like the first woman, who ate the apple and led us men into the sins of the flesh, eh?' Ruggiero gave a lascivious smile.

He was still holding onto her hand. Eve tried to pull away, but he held on just for a moment too long before letting it go.

'All right, Ruggiero, you've had your fun,' Wyatt said, approaching and taking Eve by the arm.

'Oh, it's like that, is it?' Ruggiero grinned.

'It's like it's none of your business,' Wyatt snapped. 'Now, unless you've come to give us productive advice or help, I suggest you leave.'

'My advice, Wyatt Bailey-Kinsey, is that you don't make the same mistake your father made.'

'What's that supposed to mean?' Wyatt said, his voice turning cold and flinty.

'The coincidence is startling, don't you think? How your father raced mine with his new prototype engine and yet crashed, and now here we are all these years later, following in our parents' footsteps. Do you have any reason to believe the result will be different this time around?'

Wyatt took a step toward Ruggiero, and Eve placed a gentle hand on his arm to hold him back.

'Are you saying I'm going to crash during the Grand Prix, is that it?' Wyatt held Ruggiero's gaze. 'That sounds very much like a threat to me.'

'Not a threat, just an observation.'

Happy stepped up beside Wyatt.

'Maybe you should quit your observationing and mind your own business.'

'And you have your trusted mechanic,

Happy Hudson, by your side,' Ruggiero said. 'Just like your father. History really is repeating itself.'

'Get out before I throw you out,' Wyatt snapped.

Ruggiero waved a languid hand towards Happy.

'No need, I think I shall leave before your handyman has another accident with his oil can.'

'Handyman!' Happy grunted from behind the cigar clamped between his teeth. 'I'll give you handyman, you jumped up little —'

'You've worn out your welcome, Ruggiero, I suggest you leave right now.'

The Italian turned to go.

'Wait a second!' Wyatt shouted after him.

Ruggiero paused with his back to Wyatt.

'First he wants me to go, then he wants me to stay, I'm in such a confused state.'

'Have you seen anyone suspicious hanging around the garages lately?'

'Suspicious?' Ruggiero slowly turned

back to face Wyatt. 'You believe your fancy new electric motor to have been sabotaged, do you?'

'Maybe,' Wyatt said.

Ruggiero said nothing. He walked out of the garage, shaking his head and chuckling.

'It's him,' Happy growled. 'He did it, I can tell. And he's laughing at us, laughing in our faces.'

'I don't know, Happy — you should be careful what you say,' Wyatt replied. 'We don't even know for certain if it was sabotage, or just a fault.'

'Wyatt, you know my thoughts on this, you've always known, and that pretentious, arrogant idiot makes me even more certain I'm right.'

'Let's not go over this again,' Wyatt said.

Happy yanked the unlit cigar from his mouth and threw it on the floor.

'It's him, I tell you.' He stomped off, muttering.

'Sorry about that,' Wyatt said to Eve.

'You've got nothing to apologise

for,' Eve replied. 'Is that man always so unpleasant?'

'To be honest, no, he's usually far worse.'

'Happy seemed upset.'

'There's a lot of history there,' Wyatt said. 'Happy was Dad's mechanic too.'

'Oh!' Eve watched Happy walking away, shoulders bowed as though in defeat. 'Was he there on the day when . . . ?'

'I'm afraid so,' Wyatt replied. 'He saw the crash, pulled my father out of the wreck. I'm not sure he's ever forgiven himself for not insisting that Dad get more thoroughly checked over.'

'That's so sad.' Eve hesitated. She knew she should be encouraging him to rest, but after finding out that his accident had been engineered and that someone was out to sabotage his place in the Grand Prix, Eve doubted he would be open to the suggestion any more than in his penthouse.

Still, she had to try.

'Wyatt, I know this is all very disturbing for you and that you want to get on with fixing your car, but the doctor said you should rest, remember?'

'Of course I remember, and that's exactly what I intend to do.' Wyatt grinned.

Eve wasn't entirely sure she trusted that grin.

'Come on, follow me,' he said, and set off almost at a run through the workshop.

'Hey!' Happy yelled. 'What about the work on the engine? You want me to fix it, or what?'

'Of course!' Wyatt shouted back. 'I can't race the Grand Prix with the car in that state, can I?'

Happy muttered something Eve didn't catch. She had the feeling it was better that way.

She followed Wyatt, trotting to keep up.

At the back of the workshop he flung open a door and stepped outside. Eve followed him and pulled up short with a gasp.

Wyatt was nothing if not full of surprises.

'Fancy a ride?' he said.

8

Eve stared at the helicopter sitting on the heliport, its rotors drooping and still.

'No, no, no, absolutely no way,' she said, shaking her head and backing up.

'Why not? It will be fun.' Wyatt grinned. 'You wanted to have a look around. This way I can show you Monaco from the best place possible, up in the sky.'

'Do you seriously think I am risking my life by getting in that tin can with you — who have suffered a head injury — and letting you fly it?'

Wyatt's smile disappeared and was replaced by a frown. 'Why not? I have my pilot's licence.'

'And you had a serious knock on the head earlier. You're meant to be resting, not flying a helicopter over Monaco!'

Eve resisted an urge to scream. How could he be so infuriating?

Wyatt's frown deepened. He obviously wasn't used to being challenged very often.

'But I find flying to be a very restful experience.'

'But what if your head injury is more serious than the doctor thought, and you collapse while we are up in the air? Remember, he said there was a risk of fainting spells! I can't fly a helicopter!'

With another casual wave, Wyatt dismissed Eve's concerns as he had earlier. 'I'm fine, honestly, you're worrying too much.' He yawned and covered it up with a hand. 'And that yawn means nothing, I'm perfectly awake and alert.'

Eve watched him stride over to the helicopter and then pause and glance back over his shoulder as he realised she wasn't following him.

'I'm not doing it.' Eve raised her hands, palms out. 'I'm not getting in that helicopter with you. You shouldn't be flying, you will kill yourself.'

'You're being ridiculous,' Wyatt said. 'There's nothing to worry about.'

Eve's insides churned. As handsome, kind, funny and clever as he was, Wyatt was driving her mad. Why couldn't he listen to reason instead of always believing he knew best?

And once again, that thought occurred to Eve; was this one of those mood changes the doctor had warned her about? Or was it his true character coming out?

'I can't stop you flying that thing,' she said, 'but if you do, you're on your own. I'm not coming with you.'

She turned to leave and almost collided with Tig. 'Oh!'

'Sorry about that,' Tig said, and looked over at Wyatt. 'Hey, why don't I take you both up?'

'You can fly a helicopter?' Wyatt said.

'Nope,' Tig replied, placing her hands on her hips and giving Wyatt a stare. 'But how hard can it be?'

'Ah, sarcasm, very good.' Wyatt walked slowly back towards Eve and Tig.

'I know you didn't hire me for my one-liners, just think of the sarcasm as an extra bonus free of charge,' Tig said, and gave Eve a brief smile.

121

Wyatt regarded Tig. 'You're full of surprises. You got your helicopter licence with you?'

'Sure.'

Wyatt looked at Eve. 'Will you come with me now, if Tig flies?'

Eve nodded, hoping her expression didn't betray the nerves she felt at the thought of getting in a helicopter.

For the next twenty minutes, she had to wait anxiously as Wyatt first checked Tig's licence and flying history, and then Tig performed her preflight checks on the helicopter. Every time the suggestion that this might not be such a good idea intruded into Eve's thoughts, she pushed it away and did her best to bury it.

But it kept fighting its way back.

'We're all set to go!' Tig yelled.

Wyatt and Eve climbed into the back seats. Seeing her nervousness, he took her hand and gave it a squeeze.

He leaned in close and whispered in her ear.

'Don't worry, you're going to love this.'

He paused. 'And . . . I'm sorry, you're right, I shouldn't be flying or even driving. I can be very stupid and obstinate sometimes. Do you forgive me?'

Eve pulled away and looked at him.

'Hmm, maybe.'

'Maybe?'

Tig started up the helicopter's engine, just as Wyatt said something else.

'What?' Eve yelled.

'You're going to love this!'

The helicopter lifted into the air, and Eve's stomach performed a perfect somersault. Wyatt, still holding onto her hand, gave it another reassuring squeeze.

Tig expertly flew them up and over the racing track. She hovered over the working area for a moment. Elijah waved excitedly up at them. Happy glanced their way and then continued with his work.

With a whoop, Tig took the helicopter into a steep, curving ascent.

Eve squeezed Wyatt's hand even harder.

'Hey, take it easy, will you, Tig?' Wyatt

yelled. 'This isn't meant to be a roller-coaster ride.'

'Sorry, boss!' Tig shouted. 'I got a bit excited.'

She levelled the helicopter's flight path out and headed inland towards the city. Eve looked out of her window, watching the ground far below rushing by.

Wyatt leaned in close to Eve so that she could hear him speak.

'How do you feel?'

Eve nodded. 'Better, thank you.'

She was still holding onto Wyatt's hand, but she didn't want to let go. He didn't seem in a rush to let go, either. She realised that the flutters of nerves had been replaced by excitement. And she wasn't entirely sure how much of that was due to flying over Monte Carlo in a helicopter, and how much was a result of holding hands with Wyatt. As they approached the conglomeration of tall luxury apartment blocks, Wyatt pointed and grinned.

'That's my apartment, can you see it?'

Eve nodded; in truth, she couldn't

make it out from all the other buildings, but hadn't wanted to disappoint Wyatt. He was like an excitable child, almost bouncing up and down in his seat.

Tig flew them over the city and down to the harbour. She soared over the yachts and out to sea, where she lowered the helicopter and skimmed it over the ocean.

Eve's grip on Wyatt's hand tightened as she stared fixedly at the water's surface rushing by, so close she thought she could lean out of the helicopter and dip her hand in it. One mistake on Tig's part and they would be in the water.

'Hey, Tig!' Wyatt shouted. 'Cut it out, will you?'

But Eve noticed he was grinning. He was definitely enjoying himself.

'Sorry, Boss!' Tig shouted, but Eve doubted she was. She looked as if she was having too much fun.

'Take us back!' Wyatt yelled. 'Over to the cathedral!'

Tig banked the helicopter and lifted them higher at the same time. Eve's stomach rolled over as the sea's green surface rushed by her window and then receded. Tig straightened them out as they headed inland.

'Down there is the Palais du Prince,' Wyatt said, pointing. 'You can tour the palace, but only when the prince is not at home.'

This time, she could see exactly what he was talking about. The palace was far too big to miss.

'That sounds awkward,' Eve said. 'How are tourists supposed to know when the prince is out? Do they just knock on the front door?'

'The flag,' Wyatt said, pointing to the courtyard turret. 'When the flag is flying, the prince is home, and when it's down, he's not. And over there is Monaco Cathedral, where Grace Kelly is buried with Prince Rainier.'

The white palace with its speckled, tiled roof faced the ocean, and Eve could not think of a lovelier place to be laid to rest. Grace Kelly had been a Hollywood actress, and starred in films directed by Alfred Hitchcock, until she married Prince Rainier and became a princess.

Wyatt leaned forward and shouted something to Tig that Eve did not catch. She banked the helicopter again, and they started descending.

'Are we going down already?' Eve said, trying to ignore the feeling that her stomach was no longer where it should be, but now located somewhere just below her feet.

'Yeah, this is boring, I've got a better idea of what we can do.'

That's pretty much what you said back in your apartment, Eve thought. Her good mood and the excitement of the helicopter ride suddenly disappeared. In fact, she was growing increasingly worried. Wyatt should be resting or at least concentrating on fixing his car, but instead he seemed intent on showing off his lavish lifestyle.

Once more she couldn't help but wonder, was this as a result of the knock on his head, or was this his true character showing itself?

Eve gripped Wyatt's hand as tight as she could when she suddenly realised they were landing. Tig expertly brought the helicopter to rest in the square in front of a golden-hued building with a domed roof and archways. Parked around them were Ferraris, and Lamborghinis, and men and women were ascending the broad steps to the palatial building.

Tig cut the engine, and the rotors gradually slowed down.

'What is this place?' Eve said.

'This is the Monte Carlo Casino,' Wyatt said. 'We're going to play the roulette wheel.'

'Oh, no, I don't think so,' Eve protested, but it was too late, as Wyatt was already pulling her out of the helicopter. 'I can't visit a casino wearing shorts and a T-shirt! Isn't there a dress code or something?'

Wyatt laughed. 'Of course there is, but that doesn't matter.'

They ran up the steps and Eve took comfort in the fact that Wyatt was dressed casually too, in shorts and a short-sleeved shirt. They strode through the grand entrance, past men and women attired rather more appropriately in suits and dresses.

A man approached Wyatt, blocking their way.

'I'm sorry, sir, but the casino has a very strict dress code, and I'm afraid —'

'Yes, yes, I know all about the dress code, thank you very much.' Wyatt looked the concierge up and down. 'You're new here, aren't you?'

The man bristled and adjusted his cuffs.

'Sir, I assure you —'

'Mr Bailey-Kinsey, how lovely to see you!' Another croupier or concierge, Eve really didn't know what to call them, bustled over.

'Neville, how are you?' Wyatt shook the older man's hand.

'Very good, sir, thank you for asking.' He turned to the first man. 'This is Mr Bailey-Kinsey, he owns the casino, and he gets to visit in whatever attire he chooses.'

The other man's cheeks reddened.

'I am so sorry —'

Wyatt clapped him on the shoulder.

'Forget about it, you were just doing your job.'

That poor man, Eve thought. *He never gets to finish a sentence.*

Wyatt took Eve by the hand once more and led her through the opulent, domed reception and into the casino proper. Lines of colourful slot machines met them, but Wyatt hurried past. After the bright sunshine outside, the casino seemed dull and gloomy, even despite the sparkling of gold trim and vibrant wall coverings.

As they approached the roulette table, a young lady walked up with a tray full of chips.

'With the compliments of the house,' she said.

This is just crazy, Eve thought. *He doesn't even have to gamble with his own money — except I suppose it is his money because he owns the casino.*

A second carton of chips was placed

on the table by Eve.

'Choose a number,' Wyatt said, as glasses of champagne were placed on the table.

'Wait, I've never played roulette before, I don't know —'

Wyatt grinned. 'Just choose a number.'

'Um, twenty-four. I think.'

Wyatt pushed a stack of green chips towards the croupier.

'Five hundred on number twenty-four,' the croupier said, and pushed the stack of chips across the roulette layout with his rake until it reached the number twenty-four. The other players called out their numbers, and the croupier pushed their chips into the appropriate spaces. Once satisfied there were no more bets, he set the wheel in motion and spun the roulette ball in the opposite direction around the outer edge.

Eve watched mesmerised as the red and black squares in the roulette wheel merged into a blur of motion. The white ball continued to whirl around the edge of the wheel, gradually slowing until it toppled inside and bounced between the ridged edges of the red and black squares.

Eve held her breath, waiting for the ball to settle onto a number; hopefully twenty-four.

The ball settled into a space.

'Nineteen, red,' the croupier announced.

'Oh, we lost,' Eve said, disappointed.

'Then we bet again,' Wyatt said.

He picked up a glass of champagne and raised it to Eve. She picked up hers and they clinked glasses.

The croupier was calling out for next bets.

Eve leaned in close to Wyatt and whispered, 'What's it like knowing that you can never lose? After all, it's your money to begin with.'

Wyatt leaned in even closer to Eve, until their foreheads were almost touching, and whispered, 'Honestly? It's kind of boring.'

'Then why do you do it?'

'I don't, usually,' Wyatt whispered. 'But I thought it might be fun tonight.'

'Monsieur Bailey-Kinsey?' the croupier said.

'Ah yes, the bet,' Wyatt said, and pushed another stack of chips towards the croupier. 'Twenty-four again, please.'

The croupier nodded and pushed the stack of chips across the cloth-covered table onto the number twenty-four. Once again, he spun the wheel and the ball in opposite directions. Eve watched, entranced. There was something hypnotic about the movement, the spinning of the colours and the motion.

The ball landed in the inner circle of the roulette wheel and bounced with a clicking noise between the ridges. Finally, it settled.

'Seventeen!' the croupier called out.

'Bad luck at the table as well as on the race track, Wyatt?'

That voice, dripping sarcasm and a sense of superiority, that Italian accent, Eve knew it could only be Wyatt's racing competitor.

But when she turned to face him, Eve realised she had been wrong. It wasn't Ruggiero, after all.

Wyatt smiled, thinly.

'Eve, may I introduce you to Calvino's father, Italo Ruggiero?'

Eve saw the likeness straight away, and they sounded just like each other, too.

Ruggiero senior took Eve's hand and gave a shallow bow. At least he didn't kiss her hand.

'Such a pleasure to meet a beautiful young woman,' he said.

'Thank you,' Eve replied, her insides squirming.

'Even through your rather drab and rather cheap and nasty clothing, your elegance and beauty shines through.' Ruggiero senior turned to Wyatt. 'Dress her up, Wyatt, and she will be a queen amongst queens.'

Eve's insides squirmed again. What was she, a fashion accessory? A dumb mannequin to be dressed up and paraded around town?

'I thought I saw your yacht in the

harbour,' Wyatt said, his voice cold and slightly hostile. 'I'm surprised that you're here, to be honest.'

Ruggiero arched an eyebrow. 'And why is that?'

'I wouldn't have thought you would want to see your son making a fool of himself in the Grand Prix,' Wyatt replied.

Eve closed her eyes. *Oh no, please Wyatt, don't antagonise him!*

'You will be the fool, Wyatt, just as your father was,' Ruggiero said. 'History will repeat itself on Saturday, when my son roars over the finish line in first place and you are left behind to be dragged from the wreckage of your car by that mechanic of yours with the ridiculous name.'

Eve sensed Wyatt stiffening beside her.

'I've already crashed once, Ruggiero. Are you telling me it will happen again on race day?'

Ruggiero paused for a moment, as though thinking through what he should say next.

'Who knows what will happen, eh?

But history suggests I will be correct, don't you think?'

'That sounds like a threat,' Wyatt replied. 'Is that what you're doing, Italo? Threatening me?'

'Don't be a fool, Wyatt. You are so blinded by your insistence on racing with these ridiculous electric engines that you are seeing enemies plotting against you when there are none. You are the threat to yourself, that is all.'

Wyatt was growing ever angrier, but his mobile rang before he could respond. He pulled it from his pocket, all the while staring at Ruggiero senior.

'Hello?' His face clouded over and he closed his eyes.

Ruggiero bowed once more to Eve, and said, 'I really must be going. Enjoy your evening.'

Eve nodded curtly in reply and watched as he sauntered away.

'No, I forgot. Yes, I'll be there.'

Wyatt rang off and looked at Eve.

'How would you like to be my guest at the Mayor's Ball?'

Eve gasped. 'No, I can't, I don't have anything to wear, and —'

'Nonsense, we can get you a dress right now.'

'But —'

'No buts, I've invited you and you've accepted. Right, we need to get a move on.'

Wyatt walked away.

Eve took a deep breath. Wyatt was kind, funny, and very handsome, but did he have to be so bossy all the time? And what about their encounter with Calvino Ruggiero's father? Didn't he want to talk about that? It was as though he had already forgotten all about it, including the possibility that his racing car had been sabotaged.

Eve couldn't keep up with his switches in mood. Was this all part of his concussion?

The doctor had told her to look out for uncharacteristic changes in mood, but how could she do that? She hardly knew him.

9

Solomon Sisters was tired and foot-sore. He'd spent most of the afternoon and the evening searching for Scott Saunders, and so far had come up with nothing. The kid had to be somewhere. He couldn't just have vanished off the face of the earth.

Sisters craned his head at the sound of a helicopter. From its ID beneath the carriage, he could see that it was Wyatt's. What was he doing flying, when he should have been resting? That boy was going to get himself killed.

Sisters chuckled at that.

He hitched up his trousers and began walking again. After all this trudging around from hotel to hotel, Sisters figured it was way past time for a drink. He knew of a tiny bar on the edge of town and off the tourist track, which suited him just fine. Tourists just annoyed him.

When he got there, the sun had set and

the lights were on. The bar was down a flight of steps, below ground level. As he suspected, the place was mostly empty. Not the kind of establishment most visitors to Monte Carlo would want to be seen in. Sisters never could work out how the place managed to make a profit. It always seemed on the edge of closing down, but it never did.

Sisters climbed heavily onto a stool at the bar. He removed his hat and placed it on the counter. He waved the bartender over.

'Whisky,' he said.

The bartender nodded, pulled a bottle from under the bar and poured dark liquid into a shot glass. Sisters picked up the glass and examined the contents, turning the glass around and around between his fingers. He looked up as he heard a commotion at the opposite end of the long, narrow basement space.

A young man had left the men's room and had been weaving his way back to his table when he bumped into a heavily muscled man wearing a vest top and covered in tattoos. Sisters suspected he was one of the men shipped in to construct the viewing stands for the Grand Prix. He rounded on the younger man.

'Watch where you're going, squirt.'

Sisters peered at the kid. He looked to be about the same age as Eve Parker. Was it possible? Could Sisters have struck lucky and found Scott Saunders after all?

Scott, if that was who he was, mumbled something to the big man. Sisters didn't catch it, but the big man did and he didn't look best pleased. He grabbed Scott by his shirt and hauled him in close to his leering face.

'You want to say that again before I snap you in half?'

Sisters sighed and climbed off the stool. It looked like his drink was going to have to wait. He ambled over to the two men.

'What do you want?' the big man growled.

Sisters looked at the younger man.

'Is your name Scott Saunders?'

He nodded, eyes wide with fear but unfocused with too much alcohol.

Sisters turned back to the bigger man.

'I'm afraid you're manhandling an associate of mine. Could you please put him down?'

'What's it to you, fatso?'

Sisters pulled a handkerchief from his trouser pocket and mopped at the sweat on his forehead. Then, without warning, he jabbed his other hand into the man's throat, his fingers locked out straight.

The big guy dropped Scott and staggered away, clutching at his throat as he struggled to catch his breath. He collapsed onto a chair, sweat popping out on his face. His crew mates gathered round.

Sisters took Scott by the arm and guided him away.

'Who are you?' Scott mumbled, his voice slurred with too much drink.

'I'm Solomon Sisters, and right now you can consider me your guardian angel.'

As Sisters passed the bar, he picked up

his drink, lifted the glass to his mouth, and tipped the whisky back in one gulp.

'Where are you taking me?' Scott asked.

Sisters guided him up the steps and out of the entrance.

'To a lovers' reunion, Scott, that's where. Now you be a good boy and come with me. I think the first thing we need to do is get you cleaned up and straightened out. I've got some things to tell you, and I need you paying attention.'

★ ★ ★

There it was again, that darker side to Wyatt's personality. He was upset and angry. It was obvious to Eve, despite how much he tried to hide it. The phone call, and the meeting with Italo Ruggiero, had been the trigger, switching his mood from funny and charming, and yes obstinate as well, to just obstinate.

When Wyatt had said he would drive them back into the city centre, Eve had reminded him that he shouldn't be driving. He had dismissed her concerns with a curt, 'Don't be silly.'

She had said no more. She had the distinct feeling that Wyatt was not about to have a discussion over this.

Wyatt drove them to a dress shop. He was silent the whole way, and Eve gave up trying to draw a conversation out of him. The stress of the last twenty-four hours had to be getting to him, Eve decided. Not only would he have pre-race nerves, but then the crash, his concussion, and now the possibility that someone had tampered with the car engine to get him out of the race.

Could Happy be right? Could it have been Calvino Ruggiero? Or perhaps it was his father, Italo Ruggiero? Or both of them?

Eve's thoughts were pushed away in a blur of activity. After considering several gowns, she chose a subtle silvery-grey dress that draped around her in soft, shimmering folds, along with strappy heeled silver sandals and a small clutch bag. Wyatt, who had been pacing up and down brooding, nodded his approval.

She freshened up at the holiday home, twisted her hair into an updo and quickly applied her make-up. Then they were then collected by a chauffeur and driven to the Mayor's Ball.

Wyatt cut just as stunning a figure in his suit as he had in a pair of swim shorts or oil-smeared overalls. Whatever he wore, wherever he wore it, Wyatt had the confidence to own it, to be his own person without regard for what anybody else might think. Eve envied him his confidence.

Sitting in the back of the limousine, as the chauffeur drove them down the twisting road through Les Moneghetti, Wyatt's mood finally began to soften.

'I'm sorry, I've acted terribly towards you for the last hour, haven't I?' he said.

'Well, maybe not terribly,' Eve replied, looking out of her window. She wasn't going to let him off that easily.

'It's Penelope, she somehow manages to wind me up without even trying. Still, that's no excuse, and I apologise.'

Eve's resolve to not let him off the hook so easily softened a little. Part of her wanted to remain angry at him for being so aloof with her, but she also felt that she needed to give him another chance. After all, she had seen a lovely, fun, generous side to him. But then something he had said to her at their first meeting came back to her; *Choose your boyfriends a little more carefully from now on, all right?*

Did that include Wyatt? Had she made the same mistake as she always did? Was he another Scott Saunders, just with more money?

'Eve? Am I forgiven?'

The limousine pulled into a wide, curving drive. The massive residence at the end of the drive glowed with lights, and Eve could already feel the excitement of the place, the hum of the party.

She gave Wyatt her most solemn stare. 'I'm not sure.'

The car slowed to a stop.

'Let me make it up to you,' Wyatt said.

'I think you've already tried that, haven't you?' Eve said, gesturing at the dress, sparkling in the lights from the façade.

Wyatt's eyes widened.

'No! Do you think I am just trying to buy my way back into your affections with gifts?' He shook his head. 'That's not what I'm doing. You needed a dress to come to the ball in, nothing more.'

'A ball you forced me into coming with you to.'

'Forced you?'

'You wouldn't let me say no!' Eve exclaimed. 'You bamboozled me into accompanying you, and it all happened so fast, and you wouldn't take no for an answer!'

Wyatt leaned forward in his seat.

'Driver, take us back please.'

'Yes, sir.'

'No!' Eve said, leaning forward too. 'We're here now, I want to go to the ball.'

Reflected in the driving mirror, Eve could see the chauffeur's eyes flicking from her to Wyatt and back again.

Wyatt shook his head.

'I was wrong to bring you, we're going back.'

'You're doing it again!' Eve snapped. 'Stop trying to make all these decisions for me. I want to stay.'

Wyatt sank back in his seat.

'You're right, I'm sorry.'

The chauffeur looked relieved that a decision had been made.

'And please stop apologising,' Eve said, and climbed out of the limousine.

Wyatt followed her. He was unusually quiet as they walked up the steps to the grand entrance. A concierge met them at the door and took their names. He led them through a vast hall and into the ballroom.

Eve gasped. Perhaps back in the car she had been feeling brave and determined, but when she saw the ballroom full of people, her nerves suddenly failed.

A string quartet played softly at the front of the hall. Men in tuxedos and women in stunningly elegant gowns danced or stood around in small groups, talking. Waiters glided between these groups, trays of champagne glasses balanced on upturned hands, replenishing drinks where needed.

'Are you all right?' Wyatt said beside her.

'Um . . .' Excitement fluttered in her stomach, battling the nerves. 'Yes, I'm fine.'

'Good,' Wyatt said, taking her by the hand. 'Let's mingle, shall we?'

Eve glanced at Wyatt. He seemed to have regained his composure after their argument in the limousine.

'There you are, at last!'

Penelope Bailey-Kinsey, or Dusty Day as she had once been known, swooped down upon Eve and Wyatt. In one hand she held an empty champagne flute and in the other a tiny plate with a single canapé on it. Her fingers were bedecked with more rings than Eve thought possible to wear at any one time, and her neck was draped in pearls and gold and sparkling stones.

Eve touched her bare neck. All of a sudden, she felt terribly out of place, even in the dress that Wyatt had so generously bought for her.

'What on earth kept you?' Penelope fussed with Wyatt's lapel and bow tie, as though he was a gauche teenager who needed tidying up.

'Hello Penelope, how are you?' Wyatt said, his tone verging on sarcasm as he brushed her hands away.

'Now, don't be like that.' Penelope plucked an invisible thread from his lapel and swatted at some non-existent fluff. 'You know how important the Mayor's Ball is. I wouldn't want you to miss out on what's sure to be an important evening.'

Wyatt leaned in to Eve.

'What my lovely stepmother is trying hard not to say, is that she needs me here so that she can show me off for her own mysterious ends.'

'Now don't be silly!' Penelope scolded, and turned her attention to Eve. 'Well, look at you.'

'Yes?' Eve replied, a sudden indignation at this woman's attitude rising to fill her chest.

'You've scrubbed up very well, haven't

you? I never would have thought there was such a beautiful little bird behind that mass of untidiness and dirt I met this morning. It's a pity you haven't worn any decoration though, you're going to stand out like a sore thumb.'

Indignation flared hot and rose to Eve's cheeks. She opened her mouth, but Penelope turned her attention back to Wyatt.

'Now, do follow me, I have some people I want you to meet.'

Wyatt arched an eyebrow. 'Actually, Penelope, I think the meet and greet can wait a little longer.' He took Eve's hand again. 'Eve and I are going to hunt down a glass of champagne each. We'll find you later.'

They walked away, leaving Penelope with a look of utter bewilderment on her face.

'That woman!' Eve muttered.

'Ignore her,' Wyatt replied. 'That's what I do, it's the best way of coping with her.'

'But why do you put up with her at all?'

'Believe it or not, beneath all that bluster and fuss, Penelope is scared and lost. Once she had her youth and beauty, but now that has all slipped away and she doesn't know how to cope. She lost her identity many years ago, and I believe she's still looking for another one.'

'You're too good to her,' Eve said.

'Maybe.' Wyatt handed Eve a glass of champagne and took one for himself. 'Thank you for looking after me today, I'm not sure you appreciate yet how much it means to me.'

'Hmm, it's not exactly a huge sacrifice for me. I've had a swim in your pool, eaten a fabulous meal, been on a helicopter flight over Monte Carlo, and now I'm at a ball wearing a dress that cost more than I earn in a month. It's my pleasure.'

Wyatt clinked his glass against hers.

'So, I'm forgiven for my tantrum earlier?'

'Of course you are.'

They both sipped at their champagne. Cold and sparkling, it tasted delicious.

Eve gazed into Wyatt's eyes. She hadn't realised how blue they were, and so deep.

'What are you thinking?' he murmured.

'That I could drink this champagne all night long, but that I'd better not or you will end up looking after me, instead of me looking after you.'

Wyatt chuckled. 'Maybe we should look after each other.'

'Would that work? I think we are both too strong-minded.'

Wyatt leaned in close. 'We could give it a try.'

Eve let him draw closer. 'I suppose we could.'

He kissed her on the lips, gently placed his arm around her and held her at the waist. She placed a hand on his shoulder. He tasted of champagne. The sound of the string quartet faded away. Eve was aware of nothing but the kiss. Of Wyatt.

She drew away, a little breathless. The sounds of the string quartet and of the couples dancing and talking rushed back.

'Is this what you meant when you said we could look after each other?' she said.

Wyatt smiled. 'It's a promising start, don't you think?'

For the first time in a long while, Eve felt comfortable and happy in the presence of a man. Which raised the question why she had put up with those other men, especially Scott, for so long? Had she really been so ignorant of what it meant to be with someone who was kind and generous and cared for you?

But at the same time, a worm of disquiet wriggled in her stomach. Wyatt was so charming and generous and lovely (and kissable) right now, it was easy to forget his erratic behaviour and sudden mood swings over the course of the day.

Choose your boyfriends more carefully from now on! The phrase haunted her.

'Penny for your thoughts?' Wyatt said.

'Hmm, I don't think so,' Eve replied. 'They're worth a lot more than a penny, so much so that even you might not be able to afford them.'

'Oh, really?' He leaned in and kissed her again. 'In that case I will have to find other means of reading your mind.'

Eve let him kiss her again. 'Is this all part of your dastardly mind reading plan?'

'Maybe, maybe not,' Wyatt murmured, drawing in for another kiss.

'Wait.' Eve drew back slightly. 'As much as I'm enjoying this, I . . .'

'What is it?' Wyatt said.

Eve sighed. 'I always rush into relationships without thinking, and here I am doing it again.'

'Eve —'

'No, don't say anything, not yet. You said it yourself this morning, when you rescued me from Scott, that I should choose my boyfriends more carefully. And you're nothing like Scott, nothing at all, but I still need to make sure that I don't keep repeating the same mistakes over and over again.' Eve paused, looking deep into Wyatt's eyes. 'Can we just take this slowly?'

'Of course,' Wyatt replied. 'Whatever

you want. And I . . .'

Now it was Wyatt's turn to sound unsure of himself.

'What?' Eve said. 'Tell me.'

'There's something I haven't told you yet, something you really should know about me.'

A chill settled in Eve's stomach. 'What is it?'

'Well, the thing is, I —'

'Now come on you two, do break up all that nonsense, this isn't the time or the place!'

Eve groaned inwardly. Penelope! Why did she always have to spoil things? What had Wyatt been about to tell her? It had sounded important. Could it be something that would change how Eve felt about him?

'Wyatt, you've met the mayor before, haven't you?' Penelope said, introducing a rotund man with a red, shiny face.

'Of course, many times,' Wyatt replied, shaking the mayor's hand.

'It's so good to see you here, we were all concerned to hear about your crash this morning.'

'Oh, it was nothing to worry about, just a little bump on the head. I'm still in the race.'

'Rafael, tell him he's being silly,' Penelope snapped. 'He shouldn't be racing tomorrow, the doctors have told him, but he refuses to listen.'

'The doctors have said this to you?' the mayor said.

Wyatt shot Penelope a glance, but smiled at the mayor. 'It was more of an advisory thing, rather than a direct instruction.' He held out his arms as though inviting an embrace. 'But as you can see, I'm here and I'm absolutely fine, never felt better, in fact.'

Wyatt swayed on his feet, and Eve grabbed him by the arm to steady him.

'Wyatt, are you all right?'

He placed a hand on his forehead.

'Yes, um, I'm fine, I told you.'

'Well, you don't look it,' Penelope said, and clicked her fingers at a passing waiter. 'You there, quick, bring us a chair, can't you see Wyatt needs help?'

Eve slipped her arm around Wyatt.

'Here, lean on me.'

She could feel the weight of him as his knees began to give way. There was no way she could hold him up if he collapsed. Where was the waiter with that chair?

Too late. Wyatt slowly crumpled. The crowd made space as Eve managed to hold on to him and at least control and slow his descent to the floor. Eve lowered herself with him until she was sitting on the dance floor and cradling Wyatt's head in her lap.

His eyes fluttered and then opened.

'What's going on?'

'You fainted,' Eve said, stroking his hair.

'Really?'

'You're too late, you silly boy!' Penelope snapped at the waiter, who had just hurried back with a chair. 'Don't just stand there, go and call for a doctor!'

'No!' Wyatt sat up. He was obviously growing stronger. 'I don't need a doctor, I'm OK.'

'My dear,' Penelope snapped, towering over Wyatt and Eve, 'that's exactly what you said just a moment ago as you crashed to the floor in a faint. Of course you're not all right. You're anything but.' She turned to the waiter. 'Now go and get that doctor.'

He made a move to leave, but Wyatt stopped him. 'I said no doctor!'

The young waiter glanced helplessly between Wyatt and Penelope, not knowing who to obey.

Penelope dismissed him with a wave. 'Just go, and leave us in peace, you silly little boy.'

Eve helped Wyatt sit in the chair.

'How are you feeling?' she said, kneeling beside him.

He gave her a reassuring smile.

'Honestly, a lot better.'

'I will leave you to recover,' the mayor said. 'Please accept my commiserations and I hope you feel better soon.'

Wyatt stared up at Penelope as the mayor disappeared into the crowd of guests.

'What did he mean by that?'

Penelope inspected her fingernails, as though she had just discovered something fascinating about them. 'Why, what do you mean? He just hopes you feel better soon.'

'Yes, I got that bit, Penelope,' Wyatt said, a hint of steel entering his voice. 'But why did he offer me his commiserations? Has someone died and you haven't told me?'

'Don't be silly.' Penelope continued inspecting her painted fingernails. 'He's simply sorry for you that you won't be racing in the Grand Prix.'

'Oh really? That's certainly news to me, who told him that?'

Eve looked away. She didn't like the direction this conversation was headed in.

'I did, of course, who do you think told him?' Penelope said. 'You can't race now, after a faint. It would be ridiculous.'

'Let me be the judge of that,' Wyatt said.

'No, I forbid you,' Penelope said. 'It's

for your own good. Imagine what would happen if you fainted at the wheel during the race.'

Wyatt stood up. 'You forbid me? It's a little late in the day to start pretending you're my stepmother now, Penelope.'

Penelope gasped and placed a hand against her cheek in a show of shock. Back when she was Dusty Day she may have been a good actress, but that certainly wasn't the case now. Eve doubted she had ever seen a less genuine display than Penelope was emoting right now.

Wyatt took Eve by the hand and they began walking away. He stumbled and put a hand to his forehead.

Eve grabbed him and led him to a chair.

'You're still not right, are you?'

'I just need a moment.' Wyatt sat down heavily.

Penelope rushed over. 'What's going on? Has he fainted again? I told you, didn't I tell you?'

A number of guests rushed over to see if they could help. A lady in a voluminous dress called to a waiter for a glass of water. A man knelt down next to Wyatt and began asking him some questions. It seemed he was a doctor.

Penelope took Eve by the arm and led her away.

'This is too much excitement for him,' she said, her voice lowered to a confidential tone. 'He should be resting, not gallivanting around town with a young woman like yourself.'

Eve was stuck for a response. Should she point out that it was Penelope, not Eve, who had insisted that Wyatt attend the Mayor's Ball? Or should she ask Penelope what she meant by the words, *young woman like yourself?*

In the end, Eve hesitated too long and Penelope spoke first.

'Wyatt is used to having his own way too much. Every night he's out, a different girl on his arm, clubs, restaurants, the casino, I'm surprised this hasn't happened before.'

'What do you mean?' Eve said, that worm of disquiet stirring in her stomach once more.

'Oh, don't be naïve!' Penelope snapped. 'Did you think he was saving himself for the 'right woman'?' Penelope crooked her fingers into quotes. 'Let's just say my stepson loves to play the field. You're not the first and you won't be the last, not by a long way.'

'Why are you saying these things?' Eve said.

'Why do you think?' Penelope arched a perfectly manicured eyebrow. 'It's about time that young man settled down, and when he does it's not going to be with a rag-tag, sackcloth would-be princess like yourself.' Penelope paused, as if waiting for her words to sink in. 'Honestly dear, it's better that you know now before you get your hopes up too much about marrying a millionaire and settling into a life of luxury.'

Billionaire, thought Eve. *He's not a millionaire, he's a billionaire.*

Penelope reached out a liver-spotted hand, her long, thin fingers bedecked with rings, and pinched a fold of Eve's softly sparkling dress. 'I suppose Wyatt bought you this? That boy has no common sense.' Penelope looked Eve up and down. 'Mutton dressed as lamb, my dear, that's what you are.'

Eve couldn't take any more. She turned on her heel and stalked back to Wyatt. He seemed to have recovered and was standing up.

He glanced at Eve, and then over at Penelope, and his expression hardened into a glare.

It had been turning into such a lovely evening as well, Eve thought, remembering the kiss. But now Penelope's words echoed around in her head, and her insides churned with tension.

10

The evening only grew worse. Wyatt decided he'd had enough of the Mayor's Ball, and Eve agreed with him. How could they stay when the tension had ramped up so much between Penelope and Wyatt?

The limousine was waiting for them outside and they made quick time back to Wyatt's home as the daylight faded and the city lights sprang into life, a soft, warm glow against the darkness.

Wyatt said nothing on the way back, and Eve left him in peace to calm down.

She couldn't get Penelope's words out of her head. Was the old woman right? Was Eve just the latest in a long line of girlfriends? A different one for every event? Like hunting and catching a prize animal and then showing it off?

Was that what Wyatt had been about to tell her, just before Penelope interrupted them? That he really was a playboy, enjoying an endless stream of parties and women? Had he suddenly experienced a flash of guilt, and a need to be honest with Eve?

There's something I haven't told you yet, something you should know about me.

The words haunted Eve, clinging to her, needling her with their unanswered question; what had Wyatt been about to confess?

If it hadn't been for Wyatt saying that, then Eve would have dismissed Penelope's words as poisonous rumour and nothing more.

But now she wasn't so sure. After all, Solomon Sisters had said exactly the same thing to her.

You're just another one in the endless line of girls our young Mr Bailey-Kinsey over there enjoys parading around town. Don't get your hopes up, young lady. Wyatt gets bored pretty easy like, and before you know it, he'll have moved on to the next girl and you'll be left behind, your head spinning, and you asking yourself just what the heck happened there.

Eve glanced at Wyatt. She didn't want him to see her looking, in case her expression betrayed her thoughts and feelings. Why should she be surprised? What had she been expecting? Wyatt had been nothing but kind and generous with her, if a little bossy at times, but they had known each other for less than a day. So why was she suddenly so jealous of all those other women?

Why was she thinking this relationship was going to be nothing more than a holiday fling for either of them?

The driver guided the limousine through the streets of Monte Carlo, alive with party-goers, dapper men and glamorous women. They oozed wealth and success, privilege and entitlement.

Eve felt as if she had been dropped onto an alien planet. She was the intruder, a different life form that could never fit in.

She tried pushing the thoughts away. She had promised to look after Wyatt, and that was what she would do. Tomorrow, her promise would be fulfilled, and she would think about how she was going to get home.

She would think about calling her parents.

As they approached his apartment Wyatt slipped his hand into Eve's and gave it a gentle squeeze.

She looked at him and he smiled at her. The turmoil of the evening, of her thoughts, began melting away at the sight of that smile.

The driver pulled to a stop in front of the entrance. They climbed out of the car and Wyatt thanked the chauffeur and watched as he drove away. They stood together on the drive and Wyatt slipped his arm around Eve's waist.

'I am so sorr —'

Eve placed her fingers against his lips. 'Shush, didn't I tell you to stop apologising?'

Wyatt kissed her fingertips. 'Hmm, I seem to remember you did.'

They stood in silence and listened to the night coming to life around them; the chirp and the buzz of insects.

Up here they could see the lights of

Monte Carlo spread out below them, and the glow of the lights on the super yachts in the harbour. Up here, above it all and in Wyatt's arms, Eve was enveloped in a sense of happiness and wellbeing. Penelope's words faded away, along with her nagging fears.

Wyatt kissed her. Eve kissed him back.

What a contrast to how she had been feeling only minutes before. Had she ever been happier?

There's something I haven't told you yet, something you should know about me.

There it was again, that confession that Wyatt had been about to make.

'Fancy a dip in the pool again?' Wyatt said.

Eve hesitated.

'Is there something wrong?' Wyatt asked.

Ask him, Eve told herself. *Ask him now what he was about to tell you earlier. Then you'll know, even if it's something you don't want to hear.*

'Eve? What is it?'

She took a deep breath.

'Back at the Mayor's Ball, you said there was something I should know about you.'

Wyatt sighed. 'Oh yes, that's right, and then Penelope interrupted us. OK, here goes.'

Wyatt took a deep breath and tipped his head back. Something caught his attention, and he frowned. 'The lights are on.'

Eve looked up at Wyatt's penthouse apartment. The windows glowed in the darkening evening.

'Someone must have broken in!' He strode for the private elevator, the doors opening as he approached.

'Wait!' Eve called, running after him. 'Don't you think we should call the police?'

The realised that wasn't going to happen. He was obviously determined to sort this out himself.

When they reached the apartment, they found it empty, but the lights were blazing and rock music pumped from the sound system. Wyatt strode across and switched off the music.

In the sudden silence that followed, they heard a splash from the swimming pool.

Eve and Wyatt looked at each other.

They both ran outside and on to the terrace, and pulled up short at the sight that met them.

'Hey, guys!' Scott shouted. 'This is amazing!'

He swam across the pool, wearing his mirrored sunglasses and looking as if he owned the place. He picked up a glass from the side and took a big swallow of his drink.

'Just what do you think you're doing?' Wyatt said, his voice as hard as a razor blade.

'I'm having a drink and just generally chilling out in your pool,' Scott replied, pushing himself back until he was floating face up in the water, and grinning. 'I love your place, it's cool.'

'Leave right now, or I'll call the police.'

'Aww, don't be like that.' Scott, floating on his back, kicked off from the side of the pool, gliding along. 'This pool's big enough for all of us.'

Eve shoved past Wyatt and strode across the patio to stand at the edge of the pool.

'What are you doing here, Scott?' she yelled. 'Is this some kind of stupid prank?'

'Come on, Eve, aren't you even a little pleased to see me?' Scott replied.

Eve wanted nothing more than to knock the stupid grin off his face. And his sunglasses. Instead of his eyes, all she could see were twin reflections of herself.

'Scott, you have no reason to be here. How did you even get in? And . . .' Eve thought for a moment. 'How did you know I was staying here?'

'Aww, babe, why don't you join me in the water and we can talk about it? Jeeves here can get us both a drink. What ho, eh, Jeeves?'

With a roar of rage, Wyatt ran to the pool and dived in, still wearing his suit. He surfaced and grabbed Scott, who retaliated with a punch.

'Stop it!' Eve yelled. 'Both of you —
stop it!'

They continued to grapple in the
water. Eve stepped back to avoid being
splashed. What was she going to do?
They were like a pair of animals.

Should she call the police? She didn't
even know the number for the emergency services in France. What about
Happy, or Tig?

Scott yelled. Wyatt appeared to be
twisting his ear. Scott grabbed a fistful
of Wyatt's long hair and yanked his head
under the water.

They were like a couple of immature
children.

There was only one thing for it. Eve
took a deep breath and let rip with a
high-pitched scream.

Scott let go of Wyatt, who surfaced.
They both stared at Eve, water dripping
from their faces.

'Thank you,' Eve said, steel in her
voice. 'Now both of you, get out of the
pool. Now.'

The two men climbed out and stood dripping, Scott in swimming shorts, Wyatt in his suit.

'Wyatt, go get some towels, Scott needs to dry off and then get dressed so that he can leave.'

Wyatt pushed wet hair off his face.

'No. I'm not leaving you here alone with him.'

'I'll be fine, please just get some towels.'

With a last warning glance at Scott, Wyatt headed inside.

Scott took a step towards Eve. She held up a hand. 'Stay right where you are.'

Scott pulled his sunglasses off.

'Eve, please, leave with me. This isn't you, you don't belong with him.'

'Is this what you came here for? To try and get back with me?' Eve shook her head. 'You're deluded, you know that? It's over between us.'

Scott's eyes narrowed.

'No, it's not. We belong together, Eve, we're right for each other. Even your mum says so.'

'What? Have you been speaking to her?'

'Yeah, I called, they're worried about you.'

'What did you tell her, Scott?'

'The truth, that you dumped me and you're hanging out with this playboy millionaire.'

Eve resisted the urge to push him back in the swimming pool. They would only have to drag him out again, or alternatively, she might jump in after him and attempt to drown him.

'That's not exactly the truth, is it?' Eve said.

Wyatt appeared on the patio with an armful of towels. He tossed one at Scott.

'What's going on?' he demanded.

'Nothing,' Eve said. 'Scott is leaving and apologises for his rudeness. Isn't that right?'

Eve's ex stared at her, clutching the towel and kneading at it. Finally, he tossed it to one side.

'This isn't you, Eve. It's not right, and

you're going to regret it.' He scooped up his pile of clothes and walked barefoot across the terrace towards the living room.

'Hey!' Wyatt called after him. 'Hey, how did you get in here, past all the security?'

'I just walked right in, man! I just walked right in,' Scott yelled, not even breaking stride.

Eve took a deep, shuddering breath. She didn't like this, not one bit.

★ ★ ★

Solomon Sisters jerked awake at the tapping on the passenger window. Scott stood outside the car, half-naked and dripping wet. Sisters unlocked the door and Scott climbed inside.

'Hey, watch out, you're getting the seat all wet,' Sisters said.

Scott sat in the passenger seat and glared. Water dripped off his head and shoulders, running down his torso and his arms.

'Oh never mind,' Sisters muttered, and sighed. 'What happened to you?'

'I thought I'd go for a dip in his pool.' Scott pulled a T-shirt over his head. 'It's a nice pool. How rich did you say that dude is?'

'I didn't.' Sisters yawned. He shouldn't have dozed off waiting for Scott, but he was getting old and tired. 'He's a billionaire.'

Scott whistled. 'Seriously?'

'Seriously.' Sisters gunned the car into life.

'So what do we do next?'

The car cruised down the road, away from Wyatt's apartment.

'Did you speak to your girl?'

'Yeah, she wants nothing to do with me, which is understandable seeing as how she's dating a billionaire now.'

'You think she's just after him for his money?'

'Of course she is. I've got no chance against a rich dude like that.'

Sisters chuckled. 'Have faith, son, there's more going on than you think.

176

You might get your woman back yet.'

'I don't know, man. I mean, I'm not sure this was such a good idea, breaking into his house and raiding his drinks cabinet.'

'You were all up for it earlier, I seem to remember.'

'Right, but I was drunk then and I'm sobering up now.'

'Maybe we should get you some more to drink, a little more fuel to juice the engine. Besides, it wasn't breaking and entering, I let you in.'

'And that's another thing, just how did you manage to do that?'

'I've got my ways,' Sisters replied.

Scott settled back into his seat.

'All right, be mysterious, I don't care. I just don't see what's in this for you. Why are you doing all this?'

'It's best you don't know, son. Let's just concentrate on splitting the happy couple up, all right? Then you can make your move back into that young lady's affections.'

'Whatever you say.' Scott closed his

eyes.

That's right, Sisters thought. *Whatever I say.*

11

The birdsong cut through Eve's dream. She and Wyatt had been on one of those super-yachts moored in the harbour, and he had sailed them away. Eve had never felt so happy in all her life. They were off on an adventure together, just the two of them, on this massive yacht all by themselves.

Except for that bird, singing its heart out.

It was a beautiful sound, but Eve wished it would fly away and stop bothering them. All she wanted was to be on her own with her man. And that's what he most definitely was now, her man.

But the bird continued singing and Eve was slowly dragged from her dream and to wakefulness. When she was conscious enough that she realised where she was, on a sofa in the living room of Wyatt's penthouse with a blanket thrown over her and a pillow beneath her head, she sat up straight with a cry.

She had fallen asleep! The excitement of the day had finally taken its toll and she had drifted off. But who had placed the blanket over her and slipped the pillow beneath her head?

Wyatt?

But he had been under doctor's orders to stay awake, and Eve had been the one tasked with making sure that happened.

'Oh!' she exclaimed, and stood up. That man was driving her mad. Why couldn't he just do as he was told?

Another thought occurred to her. What if Wyatt had also fallen asleep?

The idea cut through her like a cold knife. For all she knew, he could be dead!

Eve ran through the villa. She found the kitchen empty, with no sign that it had been used since last night. She ran up the stairs and threw open the doors to the bedrooms one by one. All empty.

Where are you, Wyatt?

She ran back downstairs and outside, on to the terrace. The surface of the pool was mottled with drops of rain, and Eve realised she was getting wet. She looked up, blinking against raindrops. The sky was heavy with dark clouds, and she heard the distant rumble of thunder.

Eve ran back inside. Where on earth could he be? She stood in the living room area, staring stupidly at the sofa with its squashed pillow and crumpled bed sheet.

Just as she was thinking about how she might get in touch with Happy or Tig, she heard a car approaching. She ran to the nearest window.

Wyatt! He climbed out of the car and made a dash for the entrance.

Eve was there to meet him when he stepped inside the apartment.

'Where have you been?' she yelled.

Wyatt held up both of his hands, in one of which he clutched a bulging paper bag.

'Whoa! What kind of greeting is that?'

Eve smacked him on the chest.

'The kind you deserve for letting me fall asleep last night when I should have been staying awake to look after you!'

'Ouch, that hurt!' He rubbed at his chest. 'Anyway, don't be like that, I tried to wake you but you were flat out.'

Eve hit him in the chest again.

'I thought you were dead!'

All of a sudden, she was close to tears.

'Hey, hey, it's OK, everything is OK.'

He took her in his arms and held her close. For a moment, she resisted him and then she gave in and sank into his embrace. She rested her head against his chest and let the tears roll gently down her cheeks.

'Did you fall asleep?' she said.

'If I say yes, are you going to hit me again?'

'I'm not sure. Maybe.'

'In that case, maybe I did and maybe I didn't.'

Eve hugged him tight. 'I'm not going to hit you any more.'

'Hmm, all right, so I might have dozed off for five minutes.'

'Only five?'

'Ah, well, let's see, I might have dozed off again after that initial five minutes for a few more minutes.'

'Right. So, how many more minutes?'

'Um, let me see, about three hundred?'

Eve let go of him and stepped back.

'Five hours? You slept for five hours?'

'And five minutes, if you count that first little doze.' He held up the paper bag. 'But before you get angry and start hitting me again, I'm fine and I got us croissants for breakfast.'

'Are you're sure you're all right?'

Wyatt grinned.

'Never felt better. Come on, I'll make us coffee and we can eat these before they get cold. They're fresh out of the baker's oven.'

'All right, I forgive you. But only because you bought croissants.'

They sat at the breakfast bar and gazed at the view from the window. The rain was falling harder, and the sea had become choppy with white-tipped waves. They saw a flash of lighting illuminate the horizon, yellow and orange against the black clouds and the dark sea. Seconds later, they heard thunder, closer than it had been.

'Did you know the weather was going to turn bad?' Eve said, sipping at the hot coffee.

'Not until this morning,' Wyatt replied. 'The forecast is bad enough that the decision has been made to postpone the Grand Prix until tomorrow. We were going to be right in the middle of the storm when we were racing.'

Eve gazed thoughtfully at Wyatt.

'You don't seem too upset.'

'I'm not,' Wyatt said. 'To be honest, it works in my favour. I'm glad of the extra time to rest and recover from yesterday.' He paused. 'And to find out who sabotaged the car.'

'Do you think you can?'

'I don't know, but I need to try. I should have been thinking about this yesterday, but I was erratic and a little hyper, I guess from the concussion.'

'I'd kind of noticed,' Eve commented wryly.

'Oh, really? How bad was I?'

Eve took his hand. 'Well, it could have

been worse, I suppose. But you did jump in the pool fully clothed and have a fight with Scott.'

'Oh yeah, I remember that.' Wyatt paused. 'Not my finest moment.'

Eve giggled. 'It was sort of funny, though.'

'I'm glad you find me a source of amusement,' Wyatt said, grinning. 'This afternoon I'll get my clown's costume out and smack myself in the face with cream pies.'

'Please don't, you're more than amusing enough just being yourself.'

'Ah, thank you . . . I think.'

'So how are we going to find out who sabotaged your car?'

Wyatt arched an eyebrow. 'We?'

'You don't think I'm going to let you play detective all by yourself, do you?' Eve said. 'Why should you have all the fun?'

'We could be a team, couldn't we? Like the Avengers.'

'Really? Like Captain America and Iron Man? I can't see myself as a superhero, and besides, those Spandex costumes would chafe something terrible.'

'No, I mean like John Steed and Emma Peel.'

'Never heard of them,' Eve said.

'All right, what about Cagney and Lacey?'

'Never heard of them, either. Starsky and Hutch?'

'Now you're talking!' Wyatt said.

'To be honest, though, we're probably more like Laurel and Hardy.'

Wyatt chuckled. 'I think you might be right.'

'So what's the plan, Stanley?'

'I think the first thing to do is return to the garage and ask around the other crews, see if any of them saw someone suspicious-looking, or a stranger who looked out of place,' Wyatt said thoughtfully. 'Someone must have seen something.'

'Have you any idea who it may have been? What about that man Calvino Ruggiero?'

'I don't know.' Wyatt paused as he thought about this. 'Ruggiero is loud and obnoxious and arrogant, but I never thought of him as a cheat.'

'He would have had the perfect opportunity though, being a familiar face around the garages.'

'Hmm, maybe, but Happy wouldn't have let him anywhere near the car.'

'And he wouldn't have let anyone else near the car, either, would he?'

'This is true. OK, maybe I will talk to Happy and the others too.' Wyatt paused. 'Before that, though, I've got to do something, and I think it might be best if you came with me.'

'Oh?' Eve narrowed her eyes. 'You're being very mysterious all of a sudden.'

'Remember last night, how I kept trying to tell you something, but we kept being interrupted?'

Eve nodded. How could she forget?

Wyatt took a deep breath. All of a sudden, he looked nervous. 'Well, I can't put it off any longer. Eve, there's something you need to know.'

Eve leaned forward, a sudden onset of anxiety twisting her insides.

'What is it?' she said.

* * *

After a shower and a change of clothes, Eve was ready. They ran outside, through the heavy downpour, and climbed into Wyatt's car. The rain thrummed a crazy, rapid beat against the roof. Wyatt switched the windscreen wipers on, but no sooner had they cleared the glass than more rain poured down to obscure the view.

'I'm so glad you're not racing in this,' Eve said.

'And it's only going to get worse later in the day,' Wyatt replied.

He drove carefully into town, through streets empty of tourists, and shops shuttered up for the day. Eve did her best to centre herself, to keep her nerves from getting the better of her.

He drove out of the city and onto the autoroute. It didn't take long before they arrived at their destination, and they pulled into the parking lot of a private airport. They dashed through the rain and into the flight centre. Outside, on the runway, a private jet plane was taxiing towards them.

Eve glanced at Wyatt. He looked preoccupied, nervous even.

The plane slowed to a halt and steps were manoeuvred into position at the door.

Eve found it difficult to see through the rain running down the window. She saw a man holding an umbrella and welcoming someone off the plane. They ran towards the flight tower, the man sheltering the passenger beneath the umbrella.

Eve lost sight of them for a moment as they entered the building, but then she saw a blur of movement as a figure dashed towards them.

'Daddy!'

Wyatt's son collided into him and wrapped his arms around him. Wyatt got down on his knees and hugged his son back.

'Hey, Jake!'
This was what Wyatt had been trying to tell her all this time. He had a son.

12

Eve sat in the back of the car while Jake took her place in the passenger seat. She watched the rain as Wyatt drove and chatted with his son in the front. The secret was out, and thankfully it had nothing to do with scores of women on Wyatt's arm, a different one every night.

He had a son. Jake was ten years old and lived with his mother, Wyatt's ex-wife, in London.

'We were married far too young,' Wyatt had said, when he had explained about Jake. 'And we just grew apart. We're friends still, but as romantic partners we weren't suited.'

'Why didn't you tell me before?' Eve said.

Wyatt frowned. 'I tried, but it was always the wrong place or the wrong time. And I was nervous. I thought you would run a mile as soon as you found out I'm a dad.'

As she watched the countryside rolling past, Eve smiled at that. All this time she had been worrying that Wyatt was a typical playboy who changed his women like other men changed their socks, and he'd been nervous about telling her that he was a responsible parent.

Eve's fears had been fuelled by Solomon Sisters and Penelope, though, and now that got Eve thinking about why they would say such things. Did they both just happen to be malicious rumour-mongers? Were their lives so sad and shallow that they would take pleasure in making other people miserable?

Jake was ten years old and looked as though he was going to grow up just as handsome as his father. When Wyatt introduced him to Eve, the boy held out his hand and shook Eve's hand formally, and with a very serious expression on his face.

'Very pleased to meet you,' he had said, and turned back to his father. 'Mummy will be pleased, she's been worried about you not having a girlfriend to share your life with.'

Wyatt had burst out laughing and held up his hands. 'Whoa, steady on Jake.' He glanced at Eve and gave her a smile. 'Eve and I are good friends, but we haven't known each other very long. We're just taking it steady for the moment.'

Jake had nodded. 'Very sensible.'

Eve had to stifle a laugh.

Now, sitting in Wyatt's car and listening to Jake chatting excitably about school and life in London, Eve felt a sense of calm settling over her. Wyatt was obviously devoted to his son, and it was lovely to see.

Such a contrast to Scott.

Maybe Eve was starting to choose her boyfriends better after all.

And who knew, maybe this was the last time she would have to choose a boyfriend at all?

Wyatt drove them to the workshop to catch up on what was happening with the repairs to the car. They dashed inside, heads lowered and shoulders hunched against the rain.

The bad weather had done nothing to deter the mechanics and the drivers, all making last-minute preparations in the hope that the race would still be on tomorrow.

'Hey Wyatt, how are you today?' Elijah said, giving Wyatt a high-five as he walked inside.

'I'm good, thanks,' Wyatt said.

And then Eve saw something incredible.

Happy broke into a grin.

'Hey, Jake! How's my little man?' he yelled.

Unlit cigar still clamped between his teeth, Happy shook hands with Jake and then gave him a massive bear hug, lifting the boy off his feet.

Jake screamed. 'Help, he's squishing me!'

'You think I'm squishing you now?' Happy demanded. 'How about this?'

And the mechanic roared with laughter.

Eve looked at Wyatt, as if to confirm to her that yes, this was the same Happy she knew, and no, he had not been stolen and replaced with an identical twin.

Wyatt grinned. 'Yeah, I know, it's amazing, isn't it? Don't worry, he'll be back to being the Happy we all know and love soon enough.'

'Oh good,' Eve said. 'Seeing him like this makes me nervous.'

Wyatt laughed and then called out to the others.

'Hey, gather round, I've got something to say.'

Tig gave Eve a warm smile. Happy frowned and let go of Jake. He chewed on his unlit cigar.

'I just wanted to say thank you for all your hard work and for putting up with me yesterday,' Wyatt said. 'I'm not sure I was quite myself.'

Happy grunted. 'Didn't notice, to be honest.'

There we go, Happy is back to his normal self, Eve thought. *That's a relief.*

'Obviously we have a serious situation here in that someone, or maybe more than one person, is attempting to cut me out of the race. We need to find out who, and more importantly, we need to make sure they don't get a second chance.'

'We're way ahead of you, Boss,' Tig said. 'One of us has been here all night, working shifts to make sure Annalise is tucked up safe and sound and secure from meddling fingers.'

'Seriously?' Wyatt's face broke into a wide smile. 'I don't deserve you guys. Thank you.'

'Is that all?' Happy said. 'I'd like to get back to work before you get all emotional.'

'Yeah, that's all,' Wyatt replied. 'Happy, why don't you show me the break in the power steering line again, I wasn't able to pay attention yesterday.'

'Come on, big fella,' Happy said to Jake. 'Let's show your dad what proper mechanics get up to.' He turned and led the way over to the car on its raised platform, with Jake by his side.

Eve remained where she was and turned to face the rain pounding the ground outside. The atrocious weather looked unlikely to relent.

'Not the kind of weather you expect in Monaco, right?' Tig said, standing beside her.

Eve laughed. 'Not really, no. Have you lived here long?'

'Nope, just the last month while I've been working with Wyatt. I'm from Australia originally.'

'You don't sound Australian.'

'I left when I was a teenager and since then I've travelled all over the place. I think my accent has a bit of everything in it these days.'

They fell silent and watched the rain.

Eventually, Eve said, 'Do you have any idea who would want to sabotage Wyatt's car? He could have died yesterday.'

'No idea at all,' Tig replied. 'I don't even know how someone could have got in here and cut the line like they did. We were here all day. But whoever it was, they knew exactly what they were doing. That line was cut just enough to work until the car got up to speed, then, wham, it snapped and the steering failed.'

'You think it might have been another mechanic?'

'It had to be. There's no way someone unfamiliar with engines could have worked that out, even with a set of detailed instructions. You need to know this stuff.'

'Do you think it might have been Ruggiero?'

Tig shrugged. 'It's possible. But if it was him, I don't know how he got inside and accessed the engine without any of us noticing. There was at least one of us of here all day.'

'Wyatt and I were thinking of talking to the other crews, see if they noticed anyone suspicious lurking around, but if you think it might be another mechanic, I'm not sure I want to any more.'

'I think maybe we should concentrate on making sure whoever it was doesn't get a second chance,' Tig said. 'And where is that creepy PI? Shouldn't he be the one guarding the car? Isn't that what Penelope hired him for?'

As if on cue, Solomon Sisters ambled

out of the rain, into the garage. Water dripped from the brim of his hat and his long overcoat was dark with damp patches.

'Oh boy, it's not just raining cats and dogs out there, but rabbits, guinea pigs and hamsters too.' Sisters pulled off the overcoat and shook it out, sprinkling water everywhere. He grinned at Eve and Tig. 'You ladies should stay inside, we don't want your hairdos getting wet now, do we?'

Tig muttered something under her breath.

Sisters removed his hat, dripping more water on the concrete floor. Hitching his trousers up, he ambled past the two women.

'What have we got here, boys?' he shouted. 'An itty-bitty little bird told me there's been some sabotaaaage.' He elongated the final word.

'That man gives me the serious creeps every time I see him,' Tig said.

'Me too,' Eve replied.

She was about to say something else

when the sound of an explosion cut her off. Eve stared wide-eyed at Tig.

'Outside!' Tig yelled, as Wyatt and Happy dashed past them.

Eve followed them. Mechanics were stumbling from a garage as smoke billowed out of it. Eve could see the orange glow of flames from inside.

Wyatt grabbed a fire extinguisher and ran to help. Happy, Tig and Elijah were right behind him.

Eve was suddenly aware of Sisters standing beside her. He seemed to have lost his usual bravado and cocky confidence. With a shaking hand, he put a cigarette in his mouth and fumbled for his lighter.

'Just what in tarnation is going on, young lady?'

Eve was asking herself the very same thing.

13

'I don't believe it!' Wyatt shouted. He sank into a chair and rubbed his hands over his face.

'What's wrong?' Eve said.

They were back in the penthouse suite. The explosion had been another team's car engine, but fortunately no one had been hurt. Wyatt had helped put out the fire and stayed behind to answer questions from the emergency crews.

Once they were allowed to go, Eve, Wyatt and Jake had returned to the apartment to clean up. Jake had then immediately jumped into the swimming pool, despite the rain.

Later that afternoon, Wyatt had received a phone call, one that he had been half expecting.

'The Grand Prix has been cancelled.'

'Oh no!'

'The committee has decided that taking into account the possibility of this being a deliberate act, it's too dangerous to hold the race tomorrow.'

Eve could see the sense in that, but she decided to keep that opinion to herself for the moment.

'Oh, Wyatt, I'm so sorry.'

'I suppose it's the sensible decision,' Wyatt said, and then punched the seat cushion. 'But who can be doing this? And why? I thought it was someone who was out to sabotage my work, but if this explosion was planned by the same people, I just don't see the logic in it.'

Eve had a thought that sent chills through her.

'Could it be . . . terrorists?'

Wyatt shook his head.

'I wondered about that too, but I don't think so. The explosion in the car engine was a small one, enough to cause damage, but not large enough to kill people. Whoever did this wasn't aiming to hurt anyone, just put the team out of action.'

Eve sat down next to him.

'Maybe it's the work of someone who hates the Alternative Grand Prix?'

Outside, the rain still fell, battering the windows and transforming the swimming pool water's calm surface into a bubbling froth.

'I just don't get it,' Wyatt said, head bowed.

Eve wanted to put her arms around him, to comfort him. He seemed so depressed. But she wasn't sure what stage their relationship was at. Had she sabotaged things already by suggesting that they go slow? And when she thought about it, last night when he kissed her he had been tired, concussed, and he'd been drinking champagne. Today he seemed like a different person, one for whom the day before might not have happened.

Maybe he couldn't remember the kiss. After all, he had fainted shortly after the first one and then slept after the second during his recovery from the concussion.

Or maybe he didn't want to remember that kiss. Perhaps he felt he had taken things too far, too fast. But that didn't fit with his image of the billionaire playboy, a different girl on his arm every night.

But that's not Wyatt, remember?
Or is it?

Eve recalled Penelope's words at the Ball.

Let's just say my stepson loves to play the field. You're not the first and you won't be the last, not by a long way.

Again, Eve wondered why Penelope would say something like that. Unless, perhaps, it was true.

She resisted an urge to scream in frustration. Why had she let that old woman get into her head and poison her thinking? Wyatt had been nothing but kind and generous to her. But she had to let him know again how she felt about him. And find out how he felt about her.

Come on, she told herself. *Don't just sit here, say something, do something!*

Start small, maybe just put your hand on his shoulder. You can do that.

Wyatt stood up and strode across to a window. Eve dropped her hand back into her lap.

'It's no good,' Wyatt said, staring out at the rain. 'I can't sit here doing nothing, I have to find out what's going on, who is behind this.'

He snatched his jacket off the back of a chair.

Eve stood up. 'I'm coming with you.'

'No, I want you to stay here,' Wyatt replied, and turned to face her. This could be dangerous.'

'Don't be silly. I'm coming with you.'

'Uh-uh.' Wyatt shook his head. He had that look on his face again, the one that said he wasn't going to be argued with. 'You're staying here, out of harm's way. Besides, I need you to keep an eye on Jake for me.'

'No way — I'm coming with you!'

'Eve, I can't let you do that, this might —'

Eve stepped forward a pace, hands on her hips. 'Hey Mister, this is the twenty-first century. Women get to vote now and everything! You can't stop me from doing anything.'

'I don't believe this. Are we arguing now?'

'Looks that way, doesn't it?' Eve's

insides filled with a familiar sense of indignation. If she was honest, she hated being told what to do as much as Wyatt did.

'Eve, you have to be the most exasperating person I have ever met!'

'Charming! I'm exasperating, am I? I guess I'm not like all the other bimbos you're used to parading around.'

'Bimbos? What are you talking about, Eve?'

'I'm talking about you and your millionaire, sorry billionaire, lifestyle. Different girl every night, was it?'

'Different girl every night?'

'Well? It's true, isn't it? I'm just the latest in a long line of girls, and I won't be the last, will I?'

'This is ridiculous! What's got into you, Eve? I don't have time for this, I need to sort out this race cancellation.'

'Fine! Just go, then, but don't expect me to be here when you get back!'

'You're going to leave Jake here all by himself?' Wyatt exclaimed.

'No, of course not,' Eve said, suddenly

feeling foolish. 'I meant, don't expect me to hang around for long when you get back, once I've finished looking after Jake.'

Now she felt even sillier.

Wyatt gave a tiny smile. 'Would you maybe hang around long enough to sort this out? Please?'

Suddenly feeling deflated, Eve sat down and let the anger drain from her body.

'Oh, I don't know. Maybe. I mean yes. It's just been such a mad couple of days, meeting you, your crash, going to that ball, the helicopter ride, the explosion, I'm not used to all this excitement.'

Wyatt sat down next to Eve and took her hand.

'I guess it has been pretty dramatic, but even so . . . bimbos? Where did that come from?'

'Last night, at the ball when you fainted, Penelope took me to one side, and —'

'That woman!' Wyatt stood up, balling his hands into fists. 'Why can't she just stop interfering with my life?' He sat down again. 'Go on, tell me, what lies did that poisonous old witch tell you?'

Eve recounted her conversation with Penelope. By the time she had finished, Wyatt looked ready to explode.

'None of what she told you is true,' Wyatt said. 'Yes, of course I have had dates come with me to various events — but a different girl every night?'

'Shush, you don't have to explain,' Eve whispered, suddenly ashamed that she had allowed herself to be drawn in by Penelope's lies.

Wyatt gazed into her eyes. 'I want to explain. By anybody's predictions, I should be a spoiled brat, living the life-style Penelope claims I am. But my father didn't bring me up that way, he taught me about civil duty, respect for others, about kindness and generosity. Qualities that Penelope does not possess a single one of.'

'What did your father see in her?' Eve asked.

'She wasn't always this way, but she

changed as she grew older and her acting career faded. There aren't many parts for older women in Hollywood. Now she just wants to live the luxury, party lifestyle of the rich and famous, but she's dependent on me for that, and I guess she sees you as a threat.'

'A threat? But why?'

'It's how her mind works. She trusts no one.'

Eve looked away from Wyatt, suddenly overcome with embarrassment that she had been taken in by Penelope's lies.

'Hey, hey, don't be like that,' Wyatt said, gently putting his hand under her chin and turning her head to face him once more. 'Penelope was an actress, remember? She's exceptional at lying, and you're not the first to be taken in by her.'

'It's just . . . I wish . . .' Eve couldn't get out what she wanted to say.

'Tell me,' Wyatt said. 'What's wrong?'

Eve bowed her head. 'It's OK, you need to go, we can talk later.'

Wyatt gently lifted her chin so that he

could see her properly.

'No, talk now. Everything else can wait.'

'Do you remember kissing me at the ball?'

'I do, and I remember thinking that it was very nice. I also remember you telling me you wanted to take things slow, that you didn't want to rush headlong into another relationship.'

'That's right, I did.' Eve paused. 'We don't seem to be having much luck, do we? If it's not Scott breaking into your house and swimming in your pool in a daft attempt at getting me back, it's your stepmother feeding me lies.'

'We don't need luck,' Wyatt said. 'We just need each other. As long as that's what you want, too.'

On impulse, Eve leaned forward and kissed him gently on the lips.

'I think it is, I'm sure it is, but . . .'

'You want to take it slow and steady, and that's fine. No one's going to break us up, OK? I'm here, and I'm not going anywhere. Not today, not ever.' He paused. 'Except, I really do have to go into town, and I really would like you to stay here. Will you, please?'

'Hmm,' Eve said. 'That was better, I suppose, at least you asked rather than ordering me.'

Wyatt cocked his head and smiled.

'Pretty please?'

'Seeing as you're asking so nicely, all right then. Besides which, I'm feeling exhausted. It must be all the excitement — and the fact that I slept on the couch last night.'

'Not very gentlemanly of me, was it, to leave you sleeping on the settee while I went to bed?'

'Yes, well, you can make it up to me when you get back. Wine, chocolates and flowers should just about do it.'

Wyatt kissed her again and stood up. 'Get some rest, the guest bedroom is all made up and ready for you. I'll be back before you know it.'

Eve watched him walk towards the front door and called out, 'Be careful!'

'Careful's my middle name!' he shouted back.

Eve awoke with a start. Rain drummed against the windows and the roof. Thunder rumbled overhead. She yawned and rubbed at her eyes. Had it been the lightning that had woken her up? The room was dark, but when Eve looked at her watch, she saw it was the middle of the afternoon.

How long had she been asleep?

She sat up in the bed, fluffing the pillows up behind her back and head. She yawned again. Sleeping during the day always seemed to make her more tired, but after the excitement of the last few days, she had needed it. She rubbed at her face, trying to wake herself up.

Twisting in the bed, she searched for the switch to turn on the bedside lamp.

A flash of lightning lit up the guest bedroom, throwing everything into relief. Shadows stood out against the bright highlights, and for a split second Eve saw the guest bedroom in high contrast, every detail popping dramatically.

Her heart seemed to stutter to a halt for a moment as she saw the dark shape of a man standing in front of the large window. The lightning lit him from behind, turning him into a silhouette.

The room fell back into darkness but still she could see him as an after-image.

Eve clutched the sheet, rucking it up in her fingers. She could hardly breathe. Her heart, which a moment ago had threatened to stop beating, was now galloping along, pounding against her ribcage.

Should she speak? Demand to know why he was here? And how did he get inside?

Slowly, her vision began to return as the harsh afterimage of the lightning flash receded. She could just make out his form, still standing in front of the window.

What was his intention? To steal from Wyatt?

Or worse than that? Maybe, to murder her?

Jake! Where was he? Had this man

done something to him already?

Her eyes flicked over to the bedside table. Where had she left her mobile? Was it in the living room? She couldn't see a house telephone.

Why didn't he move?

'Eve.'

Relief flooded through her.

'Scott!' she hissed. 'What on earth are you doing? You scared me!' Thunder rumbled and crashed. It seemed to Eve that a shiver ran through her torso.

She found the switch for the bedside lamp.

'Oh, Scott,' she said.

Rainwater dripped from his chin and his hands, hanging loose by his sides. A puddle had formed at his feet on the tiled floor. He couldn't have been any wetter if he had gone for a swim again.

Eve climbed off the bed. 'You've got to stop this! You can't just break into people's homes, you'll get arrested.' She walked towards the bedroom door, intending to get Scott a towel.

'Wait!' he said.

Eve turned. And she froze.
Scott was pointing a gun right at her.

14

Thunder rumbled overhead. If this had been a movie, then Eve would not have believed it, and laughed out loud at the ridiculousness of it all. A man clutching a gun, standing in the open French doors, the curtains billowing around him in the wind, and thunder rolling above them.

But it wasn't a movie; this was deadly reality.

Eve wanted to speak, to ask Scott what he was doing, but her mouth had turned dry. If she tried to say something, she doubted she could manage anything more than a strangled croak. But she had to say something. How long could they both stand here?

A flash of lightning lit up the room, and threw Scott's features into harsh relief. Was it a trick of the light, or did he look wild-eyed and crazy? A curtain blew inside and flapped across him, hiding him from view for a moment. It had blown back again before Eve could think about running.

She worked some saliva into her mouth. There had to be something she could say to him to calm him down, to persuade him to lower the gun.

'Scott . . .' No good, she sounded like a frog with a sore throat. She had to try again. 'Scott, please, what are you doing?'

More thunder rumbled in the heavy sky, and outside the rain began falling even harder.

'Please, Scott, put the gun down, please.'

Another burst of lightning, like crazy strobe lighting at a concert or in a club. The storm had to be right over them. A strong gust of wind blew the curtains inside, along with the rain. One of the large curtains flapped in front of Scott once more, covering him. This time it stayed in place a moment longer, and he was an outline beneath the curtain material flapping in the wind.

Eve turned and bolted for the bed-room door.

She heard Scott yelling, something incoherent but filled with rage.

Eve slammed the bedroom door behind her, wishing it had a lock Where was Jake? Would he still be in the living room area, or had he gone to his bedroom too?

Or had Scott already found him and done something terrible to the boy?

Eve flung open Jake's bedroom door, but his room was empty. Her insides twisted with anxiety.

She heard the guest bedroom door being thrown open with a crash.

'Eve!' Scott roared.

Eve turned and froze.

Scott advanced upon her, the gun in his hand. He held it by his side, almost as though he had forgotten it. For once he wasn't wearing his mirrored sunglasses and his eyes were unfocused, almost as though he was looking at something else other than Eve.

'Scott, please, what are you doing?' she said.

'You've been cheating on me, Eve.

Cheating on me with that playboy.'

His voice was slurred. Was he drunk? Had he just been prowling the bars of Monte Carlo since she had thrown him out last night?

'No, Scott, I haven't been cheating on you.' Eve worked to keep her voice steady. 'We broke up, you and me. We're not an item any more.'

Scott shook his head. 'That's not true, it's him, that playboy, he's lying to you, Eve. He doesn't love you, not like me.' His head drooped. 'Not like me.'

Keep him talking, Eve thought. *He's had too much to drink, and he's tired, exhausted even. Keep him talking and get that gun off him.*

'Scott, I'm so sorry, I really am, but you can't do this.' Eve slowly approached him. 'Look at you, you're so tired you can barely stand up.' She drew closer, almost within touching distance. 'Let me help you, Scott.'

She was so close now that she could reach out and take the gun if he would let her. He seemed calm, resigned even.

Maybe he had come to his senses and realised what he had done.

Eve reached out slowly, taking her time, not wanting to disturb him with any sudden moves.

'Eve? I heard a shout, what's happening?'

Jake was standing behind Scott, his eyes wide with fear as he suddenly noticed the gun.

At the sound of the boy's voice, Scott jerked to life. He spun around and fired the gun, its sharp crack deafening Eve for a moment.

Eve screamed. A window shattered, scattering glass across the floor. The sharp crack of the pistol echoed in her ears still.

'Jake!' Eve screamed.

Had he been hit? She saw him lying face down on the floor. Her heart hammered in her chest as she stared at his small body.

'No, I didn't mean to!' Scott wailed, clutching at his forehead. 'I'm sorry, it's not my fault!'

Jake suddenly leapt to his feet and ran. He was all right! He must have dived to the floor when he heard the shot. He dashed down the stairs to the next floor and Eve heard him slam a door shut.

Scott, his back to Eve, stared after the boy.

Filled with a sudden rage, Eve launched herself at Scott. She smacked into him and made a grab for his gun. He snatched it out of her reach as they both fell. Scott landed on his back in the shards of glass from the shattered window, and cried out in pain or anger, Eve wasn't sure.

The unfocused, dazed look in his eyes had been replaced with a fierce wildness. Eve realised he wasn't holding the gun any more; he must have dropped it when he smacked against the floor.

She scrambled to her feet. Scott seemed to have grown extra arms and grabbed at her. Eve tried squirming out of his grip, but he was too fast and too strong. He pulled her down with him and she fell on top of him. For a moment, she had a hand free, and she slapped him across the face.

The sting of the slap shocked Scott into letting her go, and she scrambled to her feet again.

She saw the gun where it had landed by Jake's bedroom door. She thought about running over and grabbing it, but she had never held a gun; she hated them, hated the thought of holding one and threatening someone with it.

Instead, she made a dash for the stairs. She had to find Jake and get them both out of here.

Scott reached out to grab her, but his hand just missed snatching at her ankle.

Eve ran down the stairs. She was almost at the bottom when lightning burst through the windows, throwing flickering shadows across her path and dazzling her.

She tripped and tumbled down the remaining steps. Her shoulder flared with pain as she hit the floor. Rolling on to her back, dazed, she saw Scott appear at the top of the stairs.

Get up! Run!

Eve's body refused to obey her mind's screamed commands. All she could do was lie there and wait while Scott slowly descended the stairs. Finally, as he drew closer and closer, she managed to convince her body to move. She dragged herself across the floor, her shoulder screaming in agony with every movement.

Scott seemed to be in a dream state. His eyes, though, betrayed the craziness in him. He stared wildly at Eve, his pupils tiny pinpoints of black.

Slowly but surely, he followed her as she dragged herself away from him. What was wrong with him? Why was he acting like this?

Eve pulled herself along the floor, not totally aware of where she was going. Scott wasn't going to let her go, but if she could distract him for long enough, then maybe Jake, if he was still here and hiding somewhere, could escape.

At the sliding door leading to the terrace overlooking the city, she managed to reach up and undo the lock. The door slid open and she was showered with rainwater. Climbing to her feet, she staggered outside. A burst of lightning, swiftly followed by a clap of thunder, made her scream. The wind tugged at her clothes and hair.

The pounding rain had drenched her from head to foot already. Water streamed down her face and her hair was plastered to her head. She blinked rainwater out of her eyes.

She had to get moving! Eve staggered across the patio, with no real idea of where she was going. Every instinct in her body was commanding her to flee, but there was nowhere to escape to.

Glancing back, she saw Scott stepping out of the apartment. His wild eyes were fixed on her.

She had nowhere left to go, she was trapped. Scott approached her, the rain running unheeded down his head and over his face. He didn't even blink the water out of his eyes.

A dark shape from the apartment

rushed at Scott and kicked him.

'Leave us alone!' Jake shouted.

Scott turned and backhanded Jake across the face. The boy tumbled to the floor with a cry. Towering over Jake, Scott raised his fist.

'Don't you dare hit him again!' Eve screamed.

She scrambled across the wet terraced floor. Scott spun around, swinging his fist and hitting her on the side of her head. Eve collapsed, slipping on the wet floor as her head seemed to split open with the pain.

Jake joined her, throwing his arms around her. They held on to each other, looking up at Scott standing over them. The rain pounded at them, drenching them.

Why hadn't Jake left when he had the chance?

Because he had stayed behind to protect Eve, just as his father would have done if he were here.

Eve hugged the boy tight, a sudden wave of affection for him flowing through her.

And a determination that she would do whatever it took to protect him.

Scott glowered down at them, clenching and unclenching his fists.

Eve realised in that moment, no matter how far they ran, he was just going to keep following them until he caught them. She could see it in the set of his body, in the fixed, crazed look on his face; he wasn't going to give up.

He was going to murder her and Jake. And there was nothing Eve could do to stop him.

15

Wyatt slowed the car to a stop outside the gate at Penelope's residence. He opened the car window and pushed the intercom button on the panel on the wall. With a buzz and a click, the gates swung open. Penelope, or one of her staff, would have seen him on the CCTV, and buzzed him through.

Wyatt manoeuvred the car along the twisting drive until the grand, faux-American house came into view. Penelope could not let go of her glory days as a Hollywood actress. She'd hardly been a leading lady, but she dined out on her brush with fame as much as she possibly could.

The front door opened as Wyatt dashed from his car to the entrance, his head bowed and his shoulders up against the torrential downpour. The maid curtsied as he shook his wet jacket.

'No need for any of that, Rita,' he said

to the young woman. He detested all these ostentatious signs of wealth, even though he was aware of his own luxury lifestyle. 'Is the lady of the house in?'

'Of course I am!' Penelope snapped, appearing from the lounge. 'Where else do you think I would be in this filthy weather?'

'And hello to you too, Penelope,' Wyatt said.

'Oh, cut the nonsense.' Penelope regarded Wyatt with an expression of, well, Wyatt wasn't entirely sure what her expression told him, but he was pretty certain it wasn't affection.

'So come on, out with it!' Penelope snapped. 'You never pay me social visits, so you obviously have a reason for being here and I haven't got all day, so please say whatever it is you've come to say and then we can both get on, can't we?'

'It's about Eve,' Wyatt said.

Penelope threw her head back and let out a short bark of a laugh. 'That silly little girl, please tell me you've dumped her.'

'As a matter of fact, I haven't,' Wyatt retorted. 'Just the opposite, but that's none of your business.'

'And what is my business?' Penelope said, her voice suddenly cold like ice.

'Nothing to do with Eve or me, especially when it comes to spreading poisonous lies about me.'

Penelope regarded her nails for a moment.

'Don't be silly, what on earth are you talking about?'

'You telling Eve that I have a different girl on my arm every night, that I am a stereotypical billionaire playboy with nothing more on his mind than meeting women and partying!'

'I said no such thing,' Penelope replied.

Wyatt shook his head in disbelief.

'You're too much. Eve told me everything.'

'And you believe her over me? Your own stepmother? Your father will be turning in his grave.'

Unable to help himself as the rage grew within his chest, Wyatt took a step towards Penelope.

'Don't you dare bring my father into this. If it wasn't for him, you wouldn't be living this lavish lifestyle.'

Penelope huffed.

'This is the thanks I get for looking after you after he died. If it wasn't for me —'

'I would have been fine,' Wyatt said. 'You only stayed so that you could get your hands on some of the money.'

Why had he come here? Why had he bothered confronting her with her lies? He should have known she would have attacked the truth with her own brand of poison.

'Wyatt, I think you should apologise to Penelope.'

Wyatt froze at the sound of that voice. It couldn't be! Surely not?

Ever so slowly, he turned to face the speaker.

'Italo, what are you doing here?'

Ruggiero senior looked very much at home, standing there holding a large glass of red wine.

'It's about time you knew,' Ruggiero said. 'Penelope and I are, what do you young people call it these days? An item, although that does make it sound as though we are something one might pop into a shopping trolley.'

Wyatt could hardly process what Ruggiero was telling him. Penelope, his stepmother, was dating the man who had once been a bitter rival of her husband?

Wyatt looked at Penelope, seeking an explanation. Penelope bowed her head and began pretending to examine her fingernails. Her usual mask of defiance and airs of superiority seemed to have slipped, revealing the bitter, yet fragile, woman beneath.

'Penelope, tell me this isn't true,' Wyatt said. 'Tell me he's joking, he's winding me up.'

Penelope jerked her head up.

'It's true.' She stared angrily at Wyatt. 'We've been together for several months now, but wanted to keep our relationship a secret. I'm sure you can understand why.'

'Oh yes, I can understand that, but what is beyond my comprehension is why you have hooked up with this sly snake of a man in the first place!' Wyatt realised he was trembling. As much as he disliked his stepmother, this still felt like a massive betrayal.

Penelope glanced at Ruggiero senior.

'He's not what you think, Wyatt. Given time, I think you will see that.'

'Oh, I think I've seen enough already.' Wyatt strode for the door, Rita the maid racing him to it so that she could open it for him.

'You can run away if you want to, Wyatt, but it changes nothing!' Ruggiero senior called after him. 'You're a failure on the race track and you're a failure in your family too.'

Wyatt hesitated at the open door, the rain sheeting inside.

'You're just like your father was, weak and insipid,' Ruggiero senior continued. 'You don't have what it takes to be a winner, you don't have the guts.'

Wyatt turned and stalked up close to

Italo. The two men glared at each other, eyeball to eyeball. Every fibre of Wyatt's being was screaming at him to punch this man in the face. He deserved it.

But he reminded himself that no matter how vindictive and nasty he was, Ruggiero was still an old man. Hitting him might be satisfying for a brief moment, but it was assault.

And Wyatt was a better man than that.

He turned and dashed through the open doorway into the downpour. He tumbled into his car and slammed the door shut. He gripped the steering wheel to stop his hands from shaking. How could Penelope have done this to him? There was no love lost between the two of them, but this went beyond that.

Had she been worried that Wyatt was going to cut off her part of his father's inheritance? The part that was dependent on her remaining his guardian? Obviously, that obligation had ended years ago, but Wyatt had never made any move to stop her from receiving the regular payments that continued to keep her lavish lifestyle afloat.

Wyatt started the car engine.

But if Penelope and Ruggiero senior were an item, as he had put it, then Penelope no longer needed Wyatt to fund her lifestyle. Italo Ruggiero could do that all by himself.

Wyatt resolved to sort out the legalities after the Grand Prix. And after that, he would be free of Penelope, and he never needed to speak to her again.

Just as he was about to drive away, Wyatt's mobile started chirping at him. The screen displayed Jake's name.

'Hey, buddy, what's up?' he answered cheerily.

His face turned white as he listened to Jake's urgent whispering.

16

They crawled on their backs across the patio, the rain lashing at their faces and their bodies. Scott swayed where he stood, as if he might fall over at any moment. What was wrong with him? Was he drunk?

Jake said something to Eve.

'What?'

Jake put his mouth against her ear.

'I called Dad. He's coming to rescue us.'

Eve kept her eyes on Scott. She was relieved Wyatt was on his way, but unsure whether he would get here in time. Scott was moving again, taking the steps slowly and carefully as he made his way past the jacuzzi towards the infinity pool.

His fists were clenched, the knuckles white from the tension.

Why was Scott doing this? They had known each other for less than a year, but Eve never would have suspected he could turn violent like this. Was her judgment of other people so bad that she would miss spotting something this obvious in someone?

Thunder rumbled overhead and everything seemed to shake, it was so close. How safe were they out here, in the middle of this thunderstorm? Could they be struck by lightning? It seemed to Eve that she and Jake would either die at Scott's hands or be electrocuted in a lightning strike.

No. Whatever else happened, Eve was going to protect Jake.

Scott drew closer. His eyes narrowed as he stared at Eve and Jake.

'Scott, please,' Eve begged, water running down her face. 'This isn't you. Please, you have to come to your senses.'

As if finally hearing Eve's words for the first time, Scott seemed to stir from a dream. The tension drained from his face. His eyes widened as he gazed down at Eve and Jake.

He lifted his head and looked at his surroundings, as if unsure of where he was and how he had got here.

'I'm sorry,' he muttered.

Eve had to strain to hear him over the wind and the rain.

'None of this was my idea. It's not my fault.'

What did he mean by that? Was there someone else here with him?

The sudden lightning flash lit up the gloomy afternoon, illuminating everything in a harsh, bright glow. Scott cried out and flung his arm across his eyes. He must have been looking right in to the lightning burst when it happened.

'Quick!' Eve hissed, grabbing Jake's arm, hauling him to his feet. 'While he's dazzled, run!'

Together, they dashed past Scott and up the steps to the apartment. Scott reached out to grab them but missed and stumbled. Eve and Jake ran inside just as another peal of thunder rumbled overhead. The building seemed to shake beneath the power of the heavens above.

Scott appeared in the patio door-way and a lightning flash behind him transformed him into a crazed monster of dark and light, and shifting shadows. Whatever momentary sanity had come over him outside, it had gone now. And the gun was back in his hand.

They had to get out, get away from him.

Before he did something stupid.

Before he used that gun on them.

Eve wrapped her arm around Jake and they stumbled for the door. Eve prayed that the elevator was waiting for them, that the doors would open as soon as she pushed the button.

'Eve!' Scott called out.

She glanced back. Scott was no longer chasing them, just standing in the living room, the gun held loosely by his side. He was crying.

'Eve, I'm so sorry, I never meant to hurt you,' he wailed.

Now wasn't the time to be having a conversation with him, Eve decided. His moods were shifting with frightening speed. She had to get Jake out, get him to safety, and then she could call the police. She backed away, urging Jake behind her.

'It's all right, Scott,' she said, trying to keep her voice level. 'I know you wouldn't hurt us, but you've got to let us go now.'

Scott regarded her from beneath hooded eyes.

'I don't know if I can do that.'

A chill swept through Eve. There it was again, another transformation from sorrow to threat. From sanity to insanity.

What was he planning on doing? Holding them hostage? Killing them? Did he even know?

The door burst open and Wyatt barged in. He took in the situation immediately and threw himself at Scott in a rugby tackle. The two men hit the floor, and the gun flew from Scott's hand and skidded across the room.

Wyatt turned Scott over so that he was lying face down on the floor and then sat on him, pinning Scott's arms behind his back.

He looked up at Eve. 'Call the police.'

Scott started crying. 'No, please.'

Eve had hold of Jake and she hugged him close. Scott had not only threatened her, but Jake, too. She could never forgive him for that, and yet at the sight of him sobbing face down on the floor, a tiny shiver of pity coursed through her chest. At least the craziness seemed to have left him now — although how long would that last?

'Don't listen to him! Call the cops!' Wyatt yelled.

Scott moaned. 'No, wait, don't call the police!'

'Are you kidding me?' Wyatt said. 'This is the second time you've broken into my apartment. I might as well just let you have the security code if I don't call the police. And you threatened Eve and Jake.'

'But I can explain, I can explain everything!'

'You sure can,' Wyatt replied. 'You can explain it all to the police when they get here.'

'Maybe we should let him talk,' Eve said.

Wyatt looked up at her. 'Are you serious?'

'I'm not saying don't call the police,' Eve said hurriedly. 'But I think we should hear what he has to say.' She paused. 'I mean, aren't you in the least bit curious as to how he got in here?'

'I guess I am at that,' Wyatt said.

He hauled Scott up and pushed him into a chair. Scott looked up at him, wide-eyed, rain dripping off his chin. A puddle gathered around his feet.

'You so much as move from that chair and I will tie you up and dangle you off the edge of the roof terrace, all right?' Wyatt glanced at Eve and Jake. 'Are you both OK?'

She nodded.

'Eve looked after me!' Jake said.

Eve almost burst out laughing. 'I don't think so, you were the one doing the protecting. I can't believe how brave you were!'

Wyatt gave Eve an appreciative nod. He turned back to Scott and glared at him.

241

'Come on then, tell us everything. And I mean everything.'

Eve went and stood by Wyatt. She regarded Scott as if he was a specimen in a jar. He was sweating and his eyes darted back and forth as though he was looking for help or a way out.

What had she ever seen in him?

'I said talk.' Wyatt's voice rang out strong and firm. He took a step towards Scott and towered over him.

Scott held up his hands. 'Wait, I'm going to talk. I'll tell you everything, just give me a moment to get my breath back.'

'Make it quick,' Wyatt said.

Scott nodded. 'OK, OK.' He gulped down some air and cast a swift glance at Eve.

'Don't go looking to Eve for any support,' Wyatt snarled. 'Now come on, out with it.'

'I wasn't going to hurt anyone, I swear!' Scott stared up at Wyatt, eyes wide and pleading. 'I just wanted to talk to Eve. I just want to . . .'

'Ask me to come back to you,' Eve said, her voice flat and emotionless.

Scott bowed his head and nodded.

'It's never going to happen, Scott. You know that, deep down you know that, don't you?'

Scott nodded. Was he crying again? Were the tears even real?

Eve felt nothing for him. Even that flicker of sympathy she had experienced a minute ago had fled, leaving an empty void.

'All right, now on to the main event,' Wyatt said. 'Just how did you manage to get past all the security and into my apartment? I don't see you as the master cat burglar, somehow. In fact, you don't look as if you could break your way into a paper bag.'

Scott mumbled something. Wyatt leaned closer. 'What did you say?'

'I had help,' Scott muttered.

'You don't say,' Wyatt said. 'Who helped you?'

Scott said nothing, refusing to even lift his head and look at Wyatt.

'You really want to go for that special view of Monte Carlo, hanging from my rooftop terrace, huh?'

Scott mumbled something.

'Again, louder this time.'

'Solomon Sisters, he let me in,' Scott said.

Wyatt stared at Eve, his mouth open. She thought of the first time she met Sisters, when he sat next to her on the sofa and asked her if she was a spy. Had he been a spy all along?

Had it been Sisters who tampered with Wyatt's car, causing it to crash?

Wyatt squatted, getting in close to Scott.

'Why? Why would Sisters let you into my apartment, not just once but twice?'

'I don't know, man,' Scott said, shaking his head. 'He just said I should tell Eve how I really feel and that I should persuade her to come back with me. He said it would work, that then she would see you for the playboy you really are and that she would come running back to me, where she belongs.'

Eve moved closer to Wyatt and Scott. 'Did you really believe all that?'

'Well, he's rich, isn't he? Isn't that why you hooked up with him?'

Eve had to fight the urge to slap Scott across the face. How dare he say these things to her when he had been the one to cheat on her?

'You're a piece of work, you know that?' Wyatt said. 'You come here to try to schmooze yourself back into Eve's affections and then you go and insult her.' Wyatt thought for a moment and then laughed. 'What am I talking about? You came here and tried to *threaten* your way back into Eve's affections. Is that how love and romance works with you, Scott? You wave a gun in a woman's face and then she comes running to you?'

Scott gave Wyatt a blank look.

He has no idea what Wyatt is telling him, Eve thought. *He is so self-centred, he can't understand the plain truth. He can't understand the dreadful, terrible mistake he has made.*

'You know,' Wyatt continued, 'I'm

interested to hear from you what you thought was going on. I mean, this man you've never met before tells you he wants to help you get your girlfriend back. Weren't you at all suspicious?'

Scott shrugged. 'I don't know, man. Maybe he has his own thing going on, but he never told me about it.'

'Unbelievable,' Wyatt said, and shook his head. 'Didn't he tell you anything at all?'

'Nah, not a thing. I overheard him talking with a couple of people, though. Man, whoever they are, they hate you so much.'

Wyatt leaned closer. 'Did you get any names?'

Scott shook his head.

Wyatt leaned back again with a sigh.

'We should call the police now,' Eve said.

'Wait a minute!' Scott looked at her, the alarm on his face plain to see. 'You said you weren't going to call the police!'

'No I didn't,' Eve replied. 'I said I just wanted to hear what you had to say for yourself. Now we've heard it, and it's time you paid the consequences for breaking and entering, and threatening me and a Jake with a gun.'

'But! But, Sisters, he let me in, that's not breaking and entering! And the gun, I . . . I never would have hurt you!'

Wyatt turned to Eve.

'I'm sorry, but I have to ask, were you out of your head when you hooked up with this guy?'

'I believe I was suffering from sunstroke,' Eve said solemnly. 'Either that or I was under the influence of a magic spell.'

'Fair enough,' Wyatt said, and picked up his mobile. 'All right, let's see what the police have got to say.'

* * *

Scott was taken away, and Wyatt and Eve were questioned by a police detective. Eve thought he had the classic look of a detective from the movies with his world-weary demeanour and his tired, sad eyes.

When he had finished, he took his leave by promising an all-out manhunt for Solomon Sisters. Wyatt thanked him, and they shook hands.

Then Wyatt got on the phone to the race organisers. With Sisters exposed as the man behind the plot against Wyatt and now on the run, maybe the Alternative Grand Prix could be reinstated again for tomorrow. After a long conversation, Wyatt finally hung up and turned to Eve with a deep sigh.

'What did they say?' she asked.

'They're going to talk with the other competitors, but if everyone agrees then yes, it's going ahead.'

'That's good news, right?'

Wyatt frowned. 'It is, but we've got an anxious wait until they've discussed it and then get back to me. Hopefully we should hear soon.'

Wyatt poured them both a glass of red wine and collapsed on the sofa. Jake cuddled up to his dad.

Wyatt ruffled his hair. 'Hey big fella,

you're a brave man, you know that?'

'No, I'm not, I was scared,' Jake said, nuzzling his head deeper into Wyatt's side.

'I know, but you still kept calm and did the right thing by calling me and sticking with Eve,' Wyatt replied. 'That's what bravery is, doing the right thing, even though it might scare you.'

Jake cuddled in even closer to his dad, and Eve had to look away for a moment. She brushed away her tears, overcome with relief that the ordeal was over, but also moved by the deep bond of love Wyatt and Jake had for each other.

'I wonder who the others were that Scott said Sisters was in touch with?' Eve said, eventually.

Wyatt stirred, as if he had been about to fall asleep.

'I was just thinking the same thing. My main competitor springs to mind, Calvino Ruggiero.'

'But why would he do this?' Eve said.

'I don't know.' Wyatt thought for a moment. 'I mean, he hates my guts, but I don't think he hates me enough to stoop to sabotage and possibly murder. I don't know, this whole thing with Scott seems to have been engineered by Sisters to put me off my game, to distract me. Is he also the one responsible for tampering with my car that day on the racetrack? And what about the explosion in Ted's engine?'

'You know,' Eve said thoughtfully, 'I was standing by Sisters that day, and he seemed genuinely shaken by that. I'd be surprised if he had anything to do with it.'

'Hey, talking about Calvino Ruggiero has reminded me, his father is now dating Penelope,' Wyatt said.

Eve sat back in astonishment. 'No way!'

'It's true, I saw them this afternoon.' Wyatt told Eve about his run-in with Penelope and Italo Ruggiero at her house.

Eve could hardly believe it.

They sat and watched the rain through the windows. Slowly it eased off until it had stopped altogether, and the clouds began to clear.

Wyatt's mobile burst into life. He snatched it up.

'Yes?' He listened for a moment. 'Thank you.'

He disconnected the call.

'Well?' Eve said.

'We're on!' he yelled and punched the air.

★ ★ ★

'This is ridiculous,' Wyatt said later, once they had calmed down. 'I should be resting, mentally preparing myself for the challenge tomorrow.'

'Why don't you go to bed?' Eve said.

'I'm too wired.' Wyatt rubbed a hand over his face. 'I've got too many questions, too much to think about.'

'Are you worried that Ruggiero might sabotage your car again?'

'No, not really. Tig and Elijah are doing a great job of taking shifts to watch over it.' Wyatt grinned. 'After the

251

race tomorrow, they will both be getting a hefty bonus in their pay.'

'Then there's not a lot for you to do, is there?' Eve said. 'The police have Scott, and they're looking for Sisters so they can question him.' She placed a hand on his shoulder. 'You just need to get some rest.'

'Maybe you're right.' Wyatt yawned and stretched out his arms. 'I think I might be more tired than I thought.'

'You should listen to Eve, Daddy,' Jake said solemnly.

Eve couldn't help but smile to herself. Jake had his *I'm-being-serious* expression on his face. He just didn't realise how cute it made him look.

Wyatt ruffled his son's hair, and said, 'Well, if you think I should go to bed too, I guess I'd better.' He yawned again. 'But still, there are so many questions left, you know? Like, is Sisters working for Ruggiero or someone else? And how did he get access to my car? And then there's that explosion —'

'Shush,' Eve whispered and placed a

finger against Wyatt's lips. 'The police can sort all that out now, it's their responsibility.'

Wyatt stifled another yawn.

'All right, all right! I'm going to bed, OK?'

Eve watched as he slowly walked to his bedroom and shut the door behind him. In the silence, she suddenly realised the rain had stopped.

'My daddy's going to win the race tomorrow,' Jake said in a matter-of-fact voice.

Eve smiled warmly at the boy.

'I know he is.'

★ ★ ★

Solomon Sisters had watched from the shadows as the police arrived and, later into the evening, left with a handcuffed Scott in their custody. The cat was well and truly out of the bag now, Sisters was sure of that. Scott would have blabbed and told Wyatt and Eve everything he knew.

Fortunately, Scott didn't know much at all; Sisters had made sure of that. But he would have told them about Sisters' involvement, which meant he had to stay hidden now, at least until the whole cat-and-mouse drama was over.

He would have preferred that it hadn't come to this so soon, but Scott had forced his hand. The little weasel had spent all day getting drunker and drunker, then he had stolen Sisters' gun and run off. Sisters had a pretty good idea where he would be headed, although he was surprised the addled Englishman could remember the security details and how to get into Wyatt's luxury penthouse.

Sisters had followed him here in time to see the police arrive.

It didn't matter. His work was almost finished, and once it was done, he would have enough cash to retire anywhere in the world he wanted. Not to mention the private jet out of the country to somewhere they didn't extricate wanted felons.

The plan was all set to be put into

motion tomorrow. As far as he could see, the whole thing was foolproof. But still, Solomon Sisters always liked to err on the side of caution.

What mattered was that Wyatt did not win the Grand Prix tomorrow. If that meant incapacitating him before he even started the race, all well and good.

Sisters' employer had no compunctions or morals; he simply wanted the job done.

And that's why Sisters was here, with the bonnet up on Wyatt's car, slicing the tiniest of nicks in the brake fluid line.

When he'd finished, Sisters quietly closed the bonnet and wiped his hands on a rag.

And he smiled with a sense of quiet satisfaction at a job well done.

17

The day of the race dawned bright and dry. The crisp sunlight gave everything a sharp, bright edge and the blue sky almost hurt to look at it.

Wyatt made breakfast for everyone, downing an energy shake of his own creation as well. He had everything down to a precise schedule; when he would eat and how much, including a finely judged balance of carbohydrates and proteins, how much water he would drink, a stretching routine and a meditation to calm his nerves.

'It's all about tuning my body just as much as Happy and Tig and Elijah have tuned the car,' he explained. 'I need to be in the right place mentally, physically and emotionally. That's something that many of the other drivers forget; competing in a driving competition, especially one as gruelling as the Monaco Alternative Grand Prix, has to be a holistic endeavour.'

He made it sound like a spiritual experience, Eve thought.

With Jake's help, she stacked the dishwasher, while Wyatt finished his preparations for the day ahead. When he was ready, they descended to the ground floor, where Wyatt opened up his garage to reveal his fleet of cars.

'Yeah, I know,' he said, pulling a face. 'It's embarrassing how many cars I have.'

Only one looked ready to be driven, the car Wyatt had been using the day he met Eve, and rescued her from Scott.

The thought of her ex sent a shiver through Eve. She could hardly believe the change that had come over him. He had been drunk last night, but also under the influence of that horrible, scheming man, Solomon Sisters.

Just what was he up to? And why?

It was out of their hands now, thankfully. Sisters was a problem for the police.

They climbed into the car, Jake in the back seat and Eve in the passenger side. The engine, rumbled into life. Wyatt eased the car out of the garage, the door rolling closed behind them.

Eve popped a pair of sunglasses on.

Wyatt picked up speed as they headed down the steep decline, taking the bends with confidence. The road snaked around the side of a hill; at times the car seemed to be clinging to the edge. On her right was a sheer drop and an amazing view of the crystal blue sea. On their left, the ground rose steeply, covered in thorny vegetation.

Wyatt had taken the car's top down, and Eve's hair blew in the wind. She caught a hint of the sea in the air, and the sun warmed her bare arms. The sun felt good, but she was glad she had smothered herself in sun cream. She was going to be outdoors for most of the day.

Eve cast a glance at Wyatt. All his concentration was on the twisting, turning road ahead. She couldn't believe how handsome he was, and how kind and generous, and brave. Never in her wildest dreams had she imagined she would date a billionaire, but here she was. And his money was the least attractive thing about him.

Eve glanced at him again. She didn't want him to feel self-conscious through her constantly looking at him, but she couldn't help herself.

She had to admit it; she was falling helplessly, head-over-heels in love. Maybe it was time to forget all this taking it slow and steady business; after all, she didn't want to lose him.

She noticed a shift in Wyatt's expression. His eyes narrowed, the skin on his face seemed to grow taut. She saw a muscle jump in his jawline.

Eve looked back at the twisting road. The car hurtled around a bend, almost skimming the crash barrier. Why was he going so fast?

'Hold on,' Wyatt said.

'What's wrong?' Eve asked.

Wyatt wrenched at the steering wheel as they took another bend far too fast for the road.

'Jake?' he called out. 'Hold on tight, OK?'

'OK, Daddy!' Jake called back.

'The brakes have failed,' Wyatt said grimly.

She saw his foot pumping at the brake pedal.

The tyres squealed against the Tarmac as Wyatt wrenched the steering wheel to the right, then to the left. Eve looked to the right and wished she hadn't. As the car screeched around another serpentine twist in the road, her vision filled with the ocean and the sky. It seemed as though they were floating above the massive drop.

The car sideswiped the crash barrier, throwing up yellow sparks. The sound of metal against metal filled the once peaceful day.

Wyatt managed to steer away from the edge, but now they were headed for the opposite side of the road. Tyres crunched against gravel. The car rocked as it bounced off the steep incline and back into the centre of the road.

Eve screamed as she heard the blast of a vehicle's horn, and saw a truck round-ing the bend, bearing down on them. Wyatt fought with the steering wheel, struggling with all his might to bring the car back under his control.

They hurtled through the narrow gap between the truck and the dirt incline. With the side of the truck towering over them on their right, and the ground rising steep on their left, for a split second they seemed to be in a tunnel.

A tunnel that was closing in on them.

Before Eve could scream again, they had shot out back into sunshine. They were hurtling right for the edge of the road, and the drop beyond it.

With a yell, Wyatt flung the steering wheel to the left and yanked the handbrake on. The car threw itself into a spin. Sky, ground, sky, ground, alternating in a dizzying swirl of movement.

The car juddered to a halt in the middle of the road. The engine had stalled and there was nothing else on the road. Apart from the ticking of the motor as it cooled, all was silent.

Wyatt's hands gripped the steering

wheel, the knuckle white.

'Is everyone all right?' he said.

'I think so,' Eve replied. Her hands were shaking. She pushed her hair out of her face and twisted in her seat. Wyatt shifted around, too.

'Jake?' he said.

Jake had the biggest smile Eve had ever seen.

'Wow! That was amazing! Can we do it again?'

18

The roar of car engines, the smell of car fuel, mechanics and drivers yelling at each other over the cacophony, all of it raised Eve's pulse, and thrills of pleasure ran through her torso. She stood with Jake, watching as the competitors in the Monte Carlo Alternative Grand Prix prepared for the twenty-eight-lap race ahead of them.

She could hardly believe they were here at last, and that Wyatt was still competing in the Grand Prix. Sitting in the car after Wyatt had wrestled it to a halt, the adrenaline slowly draining from her body, Eve had thought he would surely cancel his involvement in the race. Someone, and that someone had to be Solomon Sisters, had cut the brake fluid line on the car.

But Wyatt had been having none of it. Despite Eve's protestations, he was determined to continue with the race.

'If I pull out now, they'll have won,' he had said through gritted teeth, as they stood with Jake by the car on the side of the road, steam pouring from beneath the bonnet.

'And if you die in a car crash on the racetrack, they'll have won then too!' Eve snapped.

Wyatt placed his hands on Eve's shoulders.

'That's not going to happen. Tig, Elijah and Happy have been taking it in turns to keep watch over the car since that first incident on the test track. There's just no way anyone could have tampered with it.'

Eve shrugged his hands off her shoulders.

'You don't know that! Maybe they've got something else in mind, something that has nothing to do with your car. Maybe they've hired a sniper to shoot you, or maybe they've poisoned you, but you won't feel ill until you're driving and then you'll crash and then —'

Wyatt placed his fingers against Eve's

lips.

'Shush. It's going to be all right.'

Eve clamped her mouth shut. She didn't want to ruin what they had, but she could feel the pressure building inside. She didn't know what she might say if she lost her self-control.

It was just that Wyatt could be so infuriating when he made his mind up about something.

'Are you all right?' Wyatt said. 'You look like you might explode.'

And then it happened. She couldn't hold it in any longer.

'Wyatt Bailey-Kinsey!' Eve yelled. 'I love you!'

She threw her arms around Wyatt and held him tight. Well, that wasn't what she had expected to say, but it felt right.

'Hey,' Wyatt replied, returning the embrace. 'I love you too.'

'Please don't die,' Eve muttered, squeezing him tighter.

'I won't, all right? I won't.'

Happy had collected them from the side of the road. He also had been concerned about Wyatt still entering the race. But he knew Wyatt well enough not to argue with him.

And now here they were, just minutes from the race start.

Eve had long since lost sight of Wyatt, but she knew he was out there. He had left her and Jake in the care of Tig, but even she had disappeared when Elijah had rushed over with news of last-minute adjustments needed on the car's engine.

The racing cars were all now lined up and ready. Among those competing today was Wyatt's arch nemesis, Calvino Ruggiero. The thought that he, and maybe his father too, had plotted to sabotage Wyatt's car sent chills through Eve. The police had spent the night looking for Solomon Sisters, but with no luck. It was as though he had simply disappeared. They had questioned Ruggiero and his father, but both denied any involvement.

'You know,' Eve had said at one point, 'don't you think it's strange that Ruggiero senior and Penelope have got together, at the same time that you are having all these problems?'

'You mean, you think they might be behind all of this?'

'Maybe. Do you think there's anything to it?' Eve had said.

Wyatt had brushed the thought away.

'Penelope is many things, but stooping to the level of sabotaging my car engine with the possibility that it might kill me is just not her.'

Eve wasn't so sure, but she had left it, not wanting to upset Wyatt hours before the race.

Tig and Elijah had reported nothing suspicious during the night, and had never let the car out of their sight. There was nothing stopping Wyatt going ahead with the Grand Prix today, even if Sisters was still at large.

But Eve didn't like it, not one bit. The thought of that man out there somewhere sent a chill through Eve. With the French police after him, though, he was no longer a danger to Wyatt.

Was he?

'Hey, how are you both doing?' Tig

said, suddenly appearing at Eve's side.

Jake gave a thumbs up. 'We're doing great!'

Eve laughed and nodded her agreement.

'How is Wyatt feeling?'

'Equal measures of excitement and nerves, I think,' Tig replied. 'They're going to be off at any minute, so I thought I'd find you two a better spot where you can watch the start.'

'That's great, thanks,' Eve said.

Tig led them through the crowds and into the stands. They had to go through security checks until finally they were in what looked like a VIP area, with a fantastic view of the starting line.

'I'll be back soon, OK?' Tig said. 'Enjoy the race!'

'Where's Daddy?' Jake said, craning his neck.

'There.' Eve pointed at Wyatt's car, Annalise, with its unique design and colouring.

Jake waved excitedly. Eve smiled, knowing that Wyatt had no chance of seeing them from his position down there. He would be in the zone now, concentrating on the gruelling race ahead, marshalling all his powers of concentration . . .

To her surprise, she saw Wyatt lift a hand and wave back.

Eve waved too, a huge smile breaking across her face. After the tension and excitement of the last couple of days, it was a relief to be here, at the beginning of this momentous race. Eve had no idea how the future would unfold, but she knew that meeting Wyatt had changed her. Never again would she choose boyfriends in haste.

But, and this thought sent another thrill of excitement through her, she probably wouldn't have to. Wyatt had made pretty clear that he wanted Eve to be a part of his life from now on, and she felt the same. She could hardly wait to see her parents' reaction when she told them she was dating a billionaire! They certainly wouldn't have to worry about her financially from now on.

A jarring klaxon pulled Eve from her thoughts. She expected the cars to pull away from their starting lines and hurtle along the road as they jockeyed for lead position, but none moved. No, that had been the signal to start the countdown. A massive digital clock on a stand had begun counting down from one minute.

The track was clear of people. The stands were packed with spectators. Engines roared as the drivers pushed down on their accelerators. Except for Wyatt. His engine, fuelled by green electricity, would be quiet.

Quiet, but extremely powerful.

The clock reached thirty seconds. A race official stood at the side of the track, holding a chequered flag out in front of him. When the klaxon sounded again to start the race, the official would also lower the flag, and the cars would roar from their starting positions.

Eve elbowed Jake playfully in his side. 'Hey, you got any idea who's going to win?'

Jake looked at her like she was talking

a foreign language. 'Daddy, of course.'

Eve laughed. 'Of course!'

She placed a hand on Jake's shoulder.

The numbers on the clock tipped over to fifteen.

Eve's insides squirmed with excitement and nerves. She wanted to wave at Wyatt again, but he would be too focused on the task ahead. Besides which, she didn't want to distract him.

The klaxon sounded again, the race marshal lowered the flag, and the cars surged forward. If Eve had thought the noise was loud before, it was nothing compared to the roar of powerful engines that swamped them now. That and the cheers from the spectators drove all else from Eve's mind as she did her best to pick out Wyatt from the press of cars disappearing around the bend.

'Wow! That was amazing,' she said as the noise subsided.

A massive monitor attached to scaffolding showed the cars racing along the track, taking the bends and jockeying for lead position. Jake squeezed Eve's hand as they watched together. He was obviously excited, but there was a long way to go yet until the race was over.

After watching the action on the screen for a few minutes, Eve suggested that they go and find a drink. The sun was blazing down, and Eve was reminded of that first day she had met Wyatt, and how hot and uncomfortable she had been.

They threaded their way through the crowds together, looking for a place to buy cold drinks.

Eve spotted Elijah in conversation with someone. She was about to raise her hand and give him a wave when something about the man he was talking to made her pause. He had his back to her, but there was something about him that looked familiar.

'Eve?' Jake said, tugging on her hand.

'Hmm?' Eve couldn't stop staring at Elijah and the mystery man. Why? What was bothering her?

The man turned his head a little.

Italo Ruggiero, Calvino's father! What was Elijah doing talking to him? Ruggiero senior was no doubt here to cheer on his son, not talk with his bitter rival's mechanic.

Elijah saw Eve and his eyes widened. Quickly finishing his conversation with the Italian, he turned and hurried away.

Ruggiero senior walked away too, without noticing her.

For one paralysing second, Eve stood wondering what to do. Then she decided to follow Elijah and ask him what was going on. She grabbed Jake's hand and pulled him with her.

'Where are we going?' Jake asked.

'Just a little detour,' Eve replied, trying her best to keep Elijah in her sights. This was proving difficult in the crowds.

'But I want a drink!'

'We'll get one, I just need to . . .'

What? What was she going to do? Corner Elijah and ask him what he was talking to Ruggiero senior about? And what if he didn't want to say? There was absolutely nothing she could do.

Another thought struck Eve, almost stopping her in her tracks.

Was Elijah a traitor, just like Solomon Sisters?

If so, had he been the one who sabotaged Wyatt's car? And had he done it again?

Eve had to stop the race. If Wyatt were to crash now, he could die.

Eve started running, dragging Jake along with her. She had to catch up with Elijah and find out what he had done.

'Eve!' Jake shouted, doing his best to keep up.

Elijah ducked beneath a handrail and disappeared beneath the stands housing the seating areas. Eve stopped at the barrier. Beneath the stands was a warren of dark passageways between the framework holding the spectator stands up. She glanced down at Jake. It was too dangerous to take him in there. Who knew what Elijah would do, how desperate he was?

No, she couldn't chase Elijah, but she could alert the race officials to the danger Wyatt was in. Eve looked from side to side.

'Eve, what are you doing?' Jake said.

'Looking for somewhere to grab a drink,' she replied. She couldn't tell him the truth, or what she suspected, it would be too upsetting for him.

There! She spotted a race official hurrying through the crowd.

'Come on!' Eve said and ran towards the man, dragging Jake behind her.

She caught up with the race official and gasped, 'Please! You've got to help me!'

'Hey lady,' the man said, turning to look at her, 'I don't have time, you'll have to ask someone else, whatever your problem is.'

Eve grabbed his arm. 'You have to stop the race, you have to stop it now.'

The man shook his head. 'Are you crazy? You're English, aren't you? Well, let me tell you, not even the Queen of England could stop the Grand Prix once it's started.'

'You don't understand, one of the cars has been tampered with, it's going to crash!'

The race marshal pulled his arm free of Eve's grip.

'Yeah right, go tell your fantasies to someone who's prepared to listen, like maybe a therapist.'

And with that, he walked away.

'Is Daddy in danger?' Jake said, staring anxiously up at Eve.

'He's going to be fine,' Eve said. 'But we just need to find someone who can stop the race.'

Eve pulled Jake along with her as she ran through the crowd, searching for another marshal, or official, of some kind. Should she call the police? They would have the power to stop the race but were they any more likely to believe her?

Suddenly, the crowd cheered as a roar of engines filled the air. Eve looked up at the nearest large screen monitor and saw the cars tearing around a bend. They had completed their first lap.

Tig! She would believe what Eve told her. And with a mechanic on her side, the race marshals were more likely to believe them.

Where would she be? The pit-stop?

Eve headed in what she hoped was the right direction. There was no time to lose, the crash could happen at any moment.

★ ★ ★

When they reached the pit-stop, Eve's heart was hammering against her chest and her face was dripping with sweat. She saw Tig sitting at a laptop with Happy and another man beside her.

Tig turned and gave Eve a wave.

Eve rushed over. 'You have to stop the race!'

Tig's smile disappeared, replaced by a look of confusion. 'What? Why should we do that?'

'This is going to sound crazy, but I think Wyatt's car has been sabotaged again!'

'Are you serious?' Happy said, his cigar shifting as he stood up.

Eve quickly filled them in on her sight-ing of Elijah with Ruggiero senior, and how Elijah had run when he had seen Eve.

The other man shook his head.

'That doesn't mean anything. There could be all sorts of reasons for what you saw.'

Tig turned back to the laptop.

'I believe her. We need to get Wyatt off the track right away.'

'And just how are you going to do that?'

'I don't know.' Tig looked up at Happy and then at Eve, her face suddenly filled with fear. 'Wyatt's communication is down, we have no way of contacting him. Happy and Bill have been trying to work out what's wrong and get it fixed.'

'You have to keep trying!' Eve rounded on the two men. 'This could be a matter of life or death for Wyatt. Can't we stop the race?'

'You're kidding, aren't you?' Bill said.

'No, she's not.' Happy chewed on his unlit cigar. 'We need to stop the race.'

'Aw, come on, Happy, you cannot be

serious! Are you telling me you believe her?'

Happy scowled at Bill. 'If Eve thinks Wyatt's car has been sabotaged, then that's good enough for me. We need to phone the head race official and stop the race right now.'

Bill rubbed at his chin.

'I'm afraid that's not going to happen. Without proof of some kind, there's no way that anyone's going to take responsibility for halting the race.'

Eve screwed her hands into fists and pushed them against her forehead. 'There has to be something we can do!'

Tig stood up. 'There is. We need to find Elijah and get the truth out of him. If we can do that, we'll have enough to get the race stopped.'

'I know where he is,' Eve replied.

'Hey Jake,' Tig said, 'you stay here with Happy, OK?'

Jake nodded, his eyes full of anxiety.

'Try not to worry, we're going to make sure your daddy doesn't get hurt,' Eve said, placing a hand on the boy's shoulder.

The two women ran out of the pit-stop, Eve leading the way to where she had last seen Elijah. Despite her words of comfort to Jake, her insides were twisted up in knots of fear.

Whatever evil plan Elijah had set up to kill off Wyatt's chances of even completing the race, the consequences could well be catastrophic.

And it could happen at any moment.

19

Eve and Tig plunged into the darkness beneath the spectator stands without a moment's pause. All that mattered right now was finding Elijah. This was no time to be scared of shadows.

But what about a man who was prepared to commit murder? Because if Wyatt crashed and died due to Elijah's tampering with the car engine, then Elijah would be a murderer. And he had to have known that, but had still gone ahead with his plan.

Eve could hardly believe it. What little she had known of the man, he had seemed pleasant and good-natured. Had she misunderstood what she had seen? Were they making a terrible mistake?

No, there could be no other possible interpretation. Elijah and Ruggiero senior had been plotting together. They had to be involved in a scheme with Solomon Sisters to discredit Wyatt and his revolutionary electric engine.

Eve and Tig crept between the scaffolding supporting the stands. Down here in the gloom, they could hear the echoes and deep thuds of the spectators shifting around above them. Eve pushed away a sudden thought, that all those spectators jammed together must weigh a massive amount. If the stands collapsed, it would mean certain death for Eve and Tig.

As they explored further, the darkness grew deeper. It seemed to cling to them like a physical thing. Tig pulled her mobile from a pocket and switched on the torch function. The tiny light was incredibly bright and lit up the metal poles and the tiered roof.

Eve was surprised to see a Tarmac surface beneath her feet. Down here she had forgotten they were in the middle of Monte Carlo and not in some underground passage, lost forever.

A clang of something, or someone, hitting a metal pole reverberated through the cavernous space. Tig swung her mobile around, catching movement in the bright light of the torch.

'Elijah!' Tig shouted, her voice echoing.

More movement, deeper in the gloom. The sound of feet running.

Above them, the crowd roared and cheered. Eve heard the racing car engines growing in power, drawing closer and closer. She froze, pinned to the spot as it seemed the racing cars must be about to slam into the spectator stands, to crash through the weight-bearing scaffolding and mow down Eve and Tig in a blaze of twisted metal.

The cars tore past, and Eve threw her hands over her ears. The roar of the cars seemed to be swallowing them up. Tig grabbed Eve by the arm and motioned away from the front of the spectator stands. She didn't seem fazed by the incredible noise and the vibrations that coursed through the ground and the scaffolding. Eve could even feel those vibrations in her chest and head.

Together, they ran between the scaffolding poles. The roar of the racing car engines faded, leaving Eve's ears ringing. Above them, the crowd cheered and stamped. Tig led the way, deeper into the gloom. The torch in her mobile lit up scraps of rubbish scattered over the ground.

Eve spotted a flash of movement ahead.

'There!' she hissed.

Tig may not have even heard her over the noise, but she had seen Eve pointing. They both ran towards the shadow fleeing from them.

'Elijah!' Tig yelled.

The general noise above them had begun to subside, and Elijah's head whipped around to stare at his pursuers. He only paused for a moment before sprinting away from them.

This is pointless! Eve thought. *We're never going to catch him.*

Elijah cried out and Eve heard a clatter of metal.

'He's fallen!' Tig shouted, and ran on ahead.

When they got to him, Elijah was lying

on his back on the ground, clutching his knee. Tig shone the mobile's torchlight in his face, which was screwed up in pain.

The two women knelt beside him.

'What have you done?' Eve yelled, grabbing him by his collar and shaking him. 'What have you done?'

'Nothing!' Elijah yelled back. 'I ain't done anything.'

'Then why have you been running away from us? Why did you run from me when I saw you talking with Ruggiero's father?'

Elijah shook his head.

'I don't know, you looked mad, I don't . . . I don't know.'

Tig pulled Eve gently off Elijah and leaned over him. 'It's been you all along, hasn't it?'

'I don't know what you're talking about,' Elijah moaned, screwing his eyes up against the bright torchlight from Tig's phone.

'You're the one who's been messing with Wyatt's engine, sabotaging it. You sliced the brake line when he crashed

on that test run, and you've done something today, haven't you? No one else
has had access to the car, and you and I
have been guarding it.'

Elijah's face crumpled. 'Yes, it was
me.'

Eve suddenly started trembling. She
folded her arms across her midriff to
stop the shaking.

'What have you done this time?' Tig
said.

Elijah closed his eyes.

'There's a small charge set to detonate
when Wyatt's engine reaches a certain
temperature.'

'*A bomb?*' Tig yanked Elijah upright,
his overalls bunched in her fists. 'You
planted a bomb in Wyatt's car?'

'It was Ruggiero's idea, he made me
do it.'

Tig shoved Elijah away and stood up.

'We need to tell the race authorities,
get them to stop the race.'

'It's too late,' Elijah said, lying on his
back on the Tarmac.'The engine temperature should reach a critical point at

any moment, and even if Wyatt turns off the engine right now, the temperature will still keep climbing for the next few minutes. That bomb is going off at any moment.'

Eve lunged at Elijah and grabbed his overalls, the material bunching up in her fists. She yanked him upright, hauling him close. Never before in her life had she felt so much hatred for someone.

Tig placed a hand on Eve's shoulder.

'Let him go, he's not worth it.'

Eve unclenched her fists and let go. Elijah fell back against the road's hot surface.

'We've got to try and get the race stopped,' Tig said. 'I'll call Bill, he'll know who to talk to. Oh no — there's no signal down here.'

Without a word, Eve turned and ran. There was no time left, they had to do something, and they had to do it now!

'Eve! Where are you going?' Tig yelled.

There was no time to explain. She sprinted through the gloom, narrowly missing the scaffolding poles as they appeared from the darkness like tall, thin ghosts. Up ahead, she could see a triangle of light where the spectator stand ended and she could get back outside.

'Eve, wait!'

Tig was right behind her, but Eve wasn't going to stop and explain. Besides, if Eve did tell her what she had planned, Tig wouldn't let her go ahead. She would tell Eve that her plan was dangerous and stupid, and she would just end up getting herself killed. And maybe Tig would be right, but it was the only chance they had of saving Wyatt.

Eve stumbled out from beneath the stands, blinking in the sunshine. She had to stop and take a moment to orient herself.

Tig pulled up beside her.

'What are you doing, Eve?' she demanded.

'Where's the nearest pit-stop?' Eve asked.

'Down this way,' Tig said, pointing.

Eve ran again, in the direction Tig had pointed. She pushed past spectators and officials, shoving anyone in her way to one side. There were a few shouts of protest, but no one tried to stop her.

Eve saw the pit-stop Tig had pointed to. As she entered, a burly mechanic stepped in front of her.

'Hey, you can't come in here,' he said.

Eve tried shoving her way past him, but he was too big, too fast, and he blocked her easily.

'You don't understand!' Eve yelled, and punched him on the chest.

'I understand you're not allowed in here, young lady.'

Eve's eyes welled up with tears. How was she going to get past him?

'Hey Brady, let her past, this is an emergency.'

Brady looked over Eve's shoulder at Tig.

'You vouch for her?'

Tig stood beside Eve. 'Yeah, let her go.'

Brady stepped to one side, although he didn't look happy about it.

Eve dashed past him, between stacks

of tyres and engine parts and startled mechanics.

There was the racetrack. A marshal stood at the side, a furled, chequered flag beside him. Eve snatched up the flag and ran out to the middle of the empty track.

'You can't go out there, you'll be killed!'

Eve glanced at the marshal headed her way, no doubt to pull her back to safety. Tig appeared and grabbed him.

'Which way are the cars racing?' Eve shouted.

Tig pointed to her right. 'From there!'

Eve could already hear them. That familiar roar of the engines growing louder. She spread her feet, planting them both firmly on the Tarmac. She held the flag out to her side, and it unfurled, revealing the black-and-white pattern.

Hundreds of faces stared at her from the stands in shocked silence.

Eve swallowed. The race had to be stopped right now, and this was the only way she could see of accomplishing that.

She just had to hope it didn't kill her, too.

Eve glanced back at Tig and the race marshal. They were arguing furiously, but Tig was standing her ground and not letting the marshal pass.

The roar of the racing engines grew steadily louder. Eve stared at the bend in the track where the cars would appear. At the broken white line running down the centre of the road, its white a contrast to the black of the Tarmac. How much longer? Only seconds, surely.

The first car appeared suddenly, shockingly. As it hurtled towards her, Eve's resolve faltered for a moment and she had to resist the urge to bolt for the safety of the pit-stop.

A tonne of metal and plastic bore down on her.

More cars followed it, screaming around that bend like a pack of mythical monsters.

Surely they had seen her now? They had to have seen the flag, at least.

Eve began waving it in front of her,

slowly from side to side, the fabric billowing and folding in on itself, before unfurling once more.

The lead car swerved and zigzagged, seemingly out of control. He was braking!

Another racing car shot past him and then spun out of control, squealing to a halt facing in the opposite direction. A third car smashed into the first, shunting it sideways.

Despite being determined to stay where she was, Eve found herself taking involuntary steps backwards. More racing cars screeched to a halt, black smoke pouring from their tyres, and leaving dark skid marks on the Tarmac.

Was that all of them? Where was Wyatt's car?

Eve stared at the mass of racing cars before her, haphazardly stopped, and black smoke drifting into the blue sky. A driver climbed out of his seat and pulled his helmet off.

Wyatt! Where was he? He was still in danger, they all were.

With a sickening lurch, Eve realised she had placed all the drivers in danger. If the bomb detonated now, while all the racing cars were packed so close to each other, the devastation would be dreadful.

The driver who had pulled his helmet off walked towards Eve.

'What do you think you're doing?'

Eve ignored him, sprinting past him and into the pack of cars.

'Everybody get out of your cars!' she screamed. 'There's a bomb, everybody run!'

More drivers climbed out of their racing cars. None of them seemed to realise how urgent the situation was though. None of them believed her.

'Run!' Eve screamed, her voice cracking with the effort.

Wyatt, she had to find Wyatt. He had to be here somewhere, there were no more cars left to screech around the bend.

'Eve?'

Wyatt! Eve turned and there he was,

standing by his car, helmet in his hand.

She ran to him. Her instincts were to throw her arms around him and hold him tight, but they didn't have time. She had to get him, get everybody, out of there.

'There's a bomb in your car!' Eve grabbed him by the hand, breathless, sweat pouring from her face. 'We have to get out of here.'

Eve would remember this moment for the rest of her life. Wyatt didn't hesitate, pause to question her or express his doubts; he acted.

'Everyone, we need to get out of here now!' Wyatt grabbed Eve's hand and pulled her with him as he broke into a run. 'Move, run!'

'Hey Wyatt, what's going on?' one of the drivers said.

'Everyone, listen up!' Wyatt shouted. 'An explosive device has been planted in my car and it is set to detonate at any moment! Let's move, get out of here!'

The other drivers took more notice of Wyatt than they had of Eve.

Wyatt grabbed Eve's arm and ran with her to the side of the track. With Tig accompanying him, he ran back onto the track to help other drivers out of their cars. As she watched them darting between the racing cars abandoned haphazardly on the road, helping each other, Eve realised there was a real community here. The competitiveness of the race had disappeared.

Soon they were gathered at a safe distance by the edge of the racetrack.

The crowd of spectators had fallen silent, and an eerie hush filled the racetrack.

Eve stared at the mass of racing cars. The ticking of the cooling engines stood out in contrast to the silence.

Had she got it wrong? Had Elijah been lying? Had this been part of the plan to stop the race?

Wyatt drew Eve close. 'Hey, are you —?'

Before Wyatt could finish his sentence, the ground shook, and the air pulsed as Wyatt's racing car exploded in a ball of fire. Fiery fragments of metal and plastic shot into the air, resembling tiny meteors as they showered the other racing cars. Eve's face grew warm from the blast of hot air that rushed over them.

The spectators screamed.

Flaming debris smashed back onto the ground and on the other cars. Fortunately, everyone was standing at a safe distance.

Wyatt wrapped his arms around Eve and held her tight as they watched the cars burning.

'Hey,' Eve heard someone say, 'that girl, she saved our lives.'

Eve closed her eyes and squeezed Wyatt tighter in an attempt to halt the shakes that suddenly consumed her.

20

How on earth had she wound up here? Eve held her hand over her eyes to shade them and gazed at the white buildings of Monte Carlo. The spectator stands and everything else associated with the Grand Prix had been taken down, and Monte Carlo looked much more like the romantic city she remembered from the Hollywood comedies she used to watch.

Eve stretched on the sun lounger, luxuriating in the afternoon sun. She even had on a new bikini.

This was the life, relaxing all day on Wyatt's superyacht, without a care in the world.

After the last few days, she needed it.

Eve took a sip of the cocktail Wyatt had made for her. They were the only two people on the yacht anchored in the harbour. The crew and the staff were returning in the morning to fit the craft out for a cruise. But for today and the rest of the evening, Wyatt had wanted it for the two of them.

Jake would be joining them tomorrow.

Eve stretched again, unable to contain the absolute joy and peace she was experiencing. She imagined herself to be like a cat, stretched out in a patch of warm sunshine.

Only a few days ago, she had been standing on the shore and looking out at the luxury yachts, wondering what it would be like to sail in one, to experience that lifestyle. And now here she was!

None of it would matter for anything, though, if it wasn't for Wyatt. Even now, on this beautiful day, the thought of how close she had come to losing him sent a chill through her. That incendiary device inserted into his racing engine would have killed him, and probably other drivers too, if it had exploded while he was racing.

Elijah had claimed he never intended to hurt anyone, that the device was meant to disable the car, nothing more. Eve wasn't sure she believed him. He was only a part of the sinister plot against Wyatt, so maybe he was telling the truth when he claimed he had been duped by those above him.

Those above him included Ruggiero senior, Solomon Sisters, and the oil companies who had employed them. Wyatt's new electric car engine, vastly superior to anything on the market right now, was a threat to the oil companies' profits. And there were certain unscrupulous shareholders prepared to resort to all manner of underhand tactics, including murder, to keep those profits for themselves.

Elijah had admitted to causing the explosion of the competitor's car too, claiming he had rigged it to throw suspicion off him. With Elijah and Tig taking turns to watch over the car, he knew that sooner or later, suspicion would have fallen on them both. With another team being targeted, it seemed that the saboteur had superhuman ways of slipping past security.

Even Sisters hadn't known about Elijah's plan, which explained his puzzlement at the time.

An investigation had been launched and arrests were being made already, including Ruggiero Senior and Penelope — drawn into the plot with the lure of wealth, and maybe even a new start for her acting career. She had provided Sisters with access to Wyatt's penthouse suite. She had also done her best to upset Eve with all her lies, with the intention of poisoning her relationship with Wyatt and distracting him from his race preparation even more.

But that was all in the past, and now here was Eve, lying in the sun aboard a luxury yacht.

The only cloud in her beautiful, deep blue sky was the fact that Solomon Sisters was still on the loose. The thought of him made her shiver.

Stop being silly, she told herself. *The police will catch Sisters soon enough.*

She took another sip of the cocktail and the straw gurgled at the bottom of the glass. Wyatt had gone to mix more drinks. Eve placed the cocktail glass on the table beside her sun lounger. She considered putting some more sun cream on; she didn't want to burn.

Eve picked up the tube of cream and squirted a blob into her palm. She rubbed her hands together and spread the sun cream over her shoulders, leaning forward and letting her hair fall over her face. She wished Wyatt would hurry up; not only was she ready for another drink, but she could do with help applying the sun cream on her back.

A footstep behind her signalled his return. She heard the clink of the glasses as he placed the new cocktails on the table.

'You're just in time,' Eve said, leaning forward even more. 'Can you rub this cream on my back?'

Wyatt's firm hands massaged her shoulders, rubbing the cream in. Fingers dug into her back.

'Hey, careful, that's a little too fierce,' Eve said, leaning further forward.

The fingers continued digging into her flesh. 'Hey, that hurts!' She turned, pushing her hair out of the way, and gasped.

'Aww, just as I was beginning to enjoy myself,' Solomon Sisters said with an ugly sneer.

Eve tumbled off the sun lounger. The brightly coloured drinks splashed across the deck, and one of the glasses shattered.

'Careful, little lady,' Sisters said. 'You don't want to go hurting yourself now, do you?'

Eve scrabbled away from him.

'Where's Wyatt? What did you do to him?'

'He's having a little nap. I thought you might like to join him.'

Sisters stepped around the sun lounger. The shards of glass crunched beneath his shoes.

Eve bumped into something solid.

He towered over her. It seemed as though his bulk was blocking out the sun. Sun cream dripped off his fingers. The thought of his hands on her made Eve feel sick.

'The police are after you.' She tried to control the tremor in her voice. 'They know everything.'

Sisters stepped closer. 'And how do you think that is going to help you right now, young lady?'

Eve had nowhere to go. She had trapped herself in a corner. The only escape route was past Sisters. What were his intentions? Was he going to murder her? Eve decided her only chance was to keep him talking.

'Why are you doing this?' she said, her voice almost breaking into a sob.

'That little stunt of yours on the race-track cost me a fair lump of cash, young lady.' Sisters rubbed a hand over his jowly chin, leaving white smears of sun cream against his pasty flesh. 'Not to mention a dent in my reputation which is going to take some time to recover.' He paused and smiled. 'I guess I just want payback.'

'What do you mean, payback?'

'Well, your boyfriend has a little cash to spare, am I right? I'm guessing he won't mind parting with some of it to get his girlfriend back.'

'You're kidnapping me?'

Sisters chuckled. 'Not my usual game plan, I must admit, but needs must and all that.'

Eve's mind whirled. But one thought surfaced; Wyatt was alive! He had to be, if Sisters was hoping that he would pay a ransom for her return.

'He won't pay you a penny!' Eve hissed. 'And you're going to jail for a very long time.'

Sisters stretched out a hand to drag her to her feet. 'We'll see. Now, you're coming with me.'

Eve's hand touched something on the floor. The other cocktail glass, the one that hadn't smashed. Clutching it tight, she swung her arm in a broad arc and smashed it against Sisters' forehead.

The big man yelled in pain, threw his hands over his face, and dropped to his knees.

Eve scrambled past him and ran.

She sprinted across the deck, heading for the railing. Eve was a strong swimmer and her intention was to dive off the yacht and swim to the quay. She would have to be careful, swimming between the massive yachts anchored there, but the alternative of staying on board with Sisters was far worse.

At the railing, she paused. It wasn't the height that put her off, it was the thought of Wyatt. If she escaped, she would be leaving him with Sisters. A furious Sisters, who may well decide to cut his losses and murder Wyatt.

Eve turned, her back against the guard rail.

Sisters was back on his feet. Blood trickled down his left temple. He stared at Eve with fury.

Kidnapping was no longer an option. Solomon Sisters was going to kill her.

Eve turned and dashed along the bulkhead. Wyatt had gone to replenish their cocktails, so had to be down in the galley. What had Sisters done when he found Wyatt? Knocked him out? Tied him up?

Eve stumbled down the broad, carpeted steps below deck. She whipped her head from side to side, searching for a clue to tell her where to go.

Sisters roared at her from the top of the steps.

She dashed through a set of double doors, shoving through them so hard they crashed against the walls and rebounded back into place.

There! She spotted Wyatt crumpled into a corner of the galley.

'Wyatt!' she called, dashing over to him.

'Huh?'

He stirred, slowly dragging his eyes open. Eve recoiled when she saw the wound on the back of his head. Sisters must have hit him with something heavy; his hair was matted with blood.

Eve grabbed him by the shoulders.

'Wyatt! Please, wake up, wake up!'

He gazed up at her with unfocused eyes. Despite the fact that his eyes were open, he still didn't look fully conscious.

Eve started at the sound of the double doors crashing open behind her. She spun around to face Sisters standing in the doorway.

'There you are,' he snarled. 'Reunited with your boyfriend, how sweet.'

'Leave us alone!' Eve yelled. 'You can't get away with this, so just leave now!'

Sisters' lips twisted into that ugly smile of his.

'I don't care any more, young lady. It's all over now, I can see that.' He rubbed at his chin, smearing more sun cream over his flesh. 'But it'll do my heart good to know that I dispatched you and Bailey-Kinsey to the afterlife. At least you'll be together, you can take comfort from that.'

He hefted a massive frying pan off the counter. A chill swept through Eve as she saw the bloodstain on its base. That was what he had used to knock Wyatt unconscious, and now he was going to use it to batter them to death.

'Eve?' Wyatt mumbled, his voice slurred.

He lifted his hands as though to defend himself, but the movement was slow and sluggish.

Eve wrapped her arms around him. 'It's all right, darling. It's all right.'

Sisters walked towards them. He swung the heavy pan, testing its weight.

Eve let go of Wyatt and slowly stood up. Behind her, on the kitchen counter, were the ingredients Wyatt had been using to make the cocktails, including a lemon sliced into quarters.

Sisters rushed at her, lifting the pan over his head and bringing it down in a fast, furious arc.

Eve snatched up a lemon quarter and shoved it into Sisters' eyes.

The pan smacked into Eve's shoulder as Sisters screamed. He dropped the pan, and it clattered against the floor. he clawed at his eyes, streaming with tears. Eve, her shoulder on fire with pain from the impact of the heavy pan, grabbed another lemon quarter and squashed it hard against his eye sockets.

Sisters screamed again. Eve shoved him with all her strength. Already unbalanced, the big man crashed to the floor.

Doing her best to ignore the pain in

her shoulder, Eve grabbed at Wyatt.

'Come on, we have to get out of here!'

Seeming more alert now, Wyatt dragged himself upright. Supporting him, Eve shuffled past Sisters who was hauling himself onto his knees and moaning. His eyes were puffy and red, and closed down to narrow slits.

'I'm going to kill you!' he roared.

Eve pulled Wyatt out into the hallway and up the stairs. The going was laborious. She glanced back, fearful of Sisters catching up with them.

The big man had stumbled out of the galley but seemed unsure of which way to go. Eve suddenly realised the lemon juice had blinded him.

Sisters snapped his head around in Eve's direction. He could still hear them. He staggered towards them and tripped on the bottom step, smacking into the stairs with a grunt.

Eve kept moving, hauling Wyatt up to the deck.

Sisters crawled up the stairs after them, grunting and gasping. He was relentless. Nothing, it seemed, was going to stop him.

Out on the deck, the sunshine hit Eve, dazzling her momentarily. Where had she left her mobile? Even if she found it, how long before help arrived? Until then, they were trapped. And how long was Sisters going to be blinded by the lemon juice for?

Eve glanced back and saw the investigator emerge. Tears streamed down his face, and he kept rubbing a hand over his red, puffy eyes.

Wyatt, still supported by Eve, groaned. Sisters jerked his head in their direction.

'Come on, Wyatt, we've got to get moving,' Eve gasped. If only he could stand up by himself; his weight was growing too much for Eve.

Together, they staggered across the deck. It was no good, they were making too much noise and hardly getting anywhere. Sisters was right behind them. He was stumbling and crashing into obstacles, but he wasn't giving up.

Eve gently lowered Wyatt to the deck.

On her own, she could move faster and quieter.

But maybe she didn't have to do either.

It was a risky plan, but it might work.

'Please, leave us alone,' she called out to Sisters, while slowly backing away.

Sisters jerked his head in the direction of her voice. Away from where she had left Wyatt.

'Come here, little girl,' Sisters snarled. 'Don't think you can hide from me forever, my eyesight's getting better all the time.'

Eve kept on backing away.

'I'm going to call the police.'

Sisters chuckled. 'No you're not, I've disabled all the phones, including your mobiles.'

Eve's bottom bumped up against the yacht's railing. There was nowhere else to go.

'You thought of everything, didn't you?' she said.

Sisters drew closer, his arms out in front like a man navigating a pitch black room. She could smell his sweat and the alcohol on his breath.

His hand brushed her cheek and he grinned.

'Ah, there you are.'

Eve smartly stepped to one side and shoved him in the back. Sisters' stomach hit the railing, and he folded over it.

For a moment he hung there, his lupper body hovering over the vast drop to the ocean. Eve planted a bare foot on his bottom and shoved.

Sisters' weight took him over the railing and he plummeted into the ocean with a massive splash. Eve sank to the deck with a sigh of relief.

21

Three days later they were back on the yacht, this time with a full complement of staff, and heading out to sea. Wyatt sported a bandage on his head, and Eve had her arm in a sling.

'What a pair we make!' Eve laughed.

They stood at the yacht's stern, watching as Monte Carlo receded into the distance.

Wyatt chuckled. 'You know, for the first time in my life, I'm glad to see the back of Monte Carlo. This time it's been nothing but trouble and aggravation. I've had two knocks on the head, I lost my senses for a while there, lost my car in an explosion, had a fight with another man in my swimming pool, fainted, and almost died.'

'Hmm, but you met me,' Eve said.

Wyatt sighed. 'Well, I suppose there is that.'

'Hey!' Eve prodded him in his side.

'What's that supposed to mean?'

'Ouch! I'm joking, I'm joking!'

'You'd better be,' Eve replied. 'I'm the best thing that's ever happened to you, mister, and don't you forget it.'

'Of course you are.' Wyatt slipped an arm around Eve's shoulders.

'Ouch, be careful!' Eve yelped as his hand brushed her bruises.

'Sorry, sorry. Is that better?'

'Yes, thanks.' Eve sank her head into Wyatt's chest. 'Seriously though, it has been pretty bad for you these last few days, hasn't it?'

'But I met you, and that made it all worthwhile,' Wyatt said.

'Flattery will get you —'

Eve couldn't speak any more because Wyatt's lips were on hers and he was kissing her.

'Aww, look at the lovebirds, aren't they cute?'

Eve and Wyatt broke apart and turned to see Happy and Tig grinning at them. Jake peeked out from behind Happy and giggled.

'Do you think they might be in love?' Tig said, her arms folded, her smile growing wider.

Happy's smile slipped, and he glowered at them, chewing on his unlit cigar. 'Yup, looks like they've got it bad, too. I think maybe we should call for medical help.'

'Hey Jake,' Tig said. 'Do you remember that song I taught you?'

'I sure do!' Jake replied, darting around Happy to stand in front of him.

Jake and Tig sang together. 'Wyatt and Eve, sitting in a tree, K. I. S. S. I. N. G!'

Clutching each other, they burst into giggles.

Wyatt gave them a slow clap. 'Very mature of you both, although Jake has an excuse due to his age. Tig, what do you have to say for yourself?'

'I'm just a big kid at heart,' she replied.

Happy was still chewing on his cigar and glowering at Eve and Wyatt.

'You know something, Wyatt?' Eve said, glowering back at Happy. 'I'm still trying to work out why you brought your

grease-monkeys with us. Aren't we supposed to be having a holiday, just the
two of us?'

Tig placed her hands on her hips.

'You haven't told her, have you?'

'I was just about to and you two interrupted!'

'What's going on?' Eve said.

'Don't be mad,' Wyatt replied. 'We're
having a holiday while we cruise over to
North Africa.'

'And then what?'

'And then I'm racing in the Sahara
Trail, a seven day endurance event across
the desert.'

'Seven days?' Eve exclaimed.

'Er, yeah, but don't worry, we'll see
each other every day.'

'Really?' Eve said. 'How come?'

A sudden, unrecognisable noise cut
through the conversation. Eve turned
and was amazed to see it was Happy
laughing.

'Because, along with me and Tig,
you're the support crew!' Happy gasped,
and slapped his thigh. 'You're gonna be

a grease-monkey!'

Tig smiled. 'Welcome aboard Team Bailey-Kinsey, Eve.'

'Welcome aboard!' Jake shouted, doing an impersonation of a pirate.

Wyatt placed an arm around Eve's shoulder and hugged her close. 'Is that all right?'

Eve looked up at him. 'Of course. It's more than alright. I love you, Mr Bailey-Kinsey.'

'I love you too, Grease-Monkey.'

And as the yacht cruised through the sea beneath the Mediterranean sun, they kissed.